MINERVA KEEN'S
DETECTIVE
CLUB

DETECTIVE CLUB

JAMES PATTERSON
AND
KEIR GRAFF

JIMMY PATTERSON BOOKS
LITTLE, BROWN AND COMPANY
NEW YORK   BOSTON

Copyright © 2023 by James Patterson
Illustrations copyright © 2023 by Alan Brown
Illustration on page 319 copyright © 2023 by Maike Plenzke

Cover art copyright © 2023 by Maike Plenzke. Cover design by Tracy Shaw.
Cover copyright © 2023 by Hachette Book Group, Inc.
Interior design by Carla Weise.

JIMMY Patterson Books / Little, Brown and Company
Hachette Book Group
1290 Avenue of the Americas, New York, NY 10104
JamesPatterson.com

Simultaneously published in 2023 by
Penguin Random House UK in the United Kingdom
First US Edition: May 2023

JIMMY Patterson Books is an imprint of Little, Brown and Company, a division of Hachette Book Group, Inc. The Little, Brown name and logo are trademarks of Hachette Book Group, Inc. The JIMMY Patterson Books® name and logo are trademarks of JBP Business, LLC.

The publisher is not responsible for websites (or their content) that are not owned by the publisher.

Little, Brown and Company books may be purchased in bulk for business, educational, or promotional use. For information, please contact your local bookseller or the Hachette Book Group Special Markets Department at special.markets@hbgusa.com.

Library of Congress Cataloging-in-Publication Data
Names: Patterson, James, 1947– author. | Graff, Keir, 1969– author.
Title: Minerva Keen's Detective Club / James Patterson & Keir Graff.
Description: First US edition. | New York : JIMMY Patterson Books, Little, Brown and Company, 2023. | Series: Minerva Keen | Audience: Ages 8–12. | Summary: "Twelve-year-old Minerva Keen forms a detective club to uncover who is poisoning residents of her storied Chicago apartment building, knowing that any one of her neighbors could be the poisoner—or the next victim." —Provided by publisher.
Identifiers: LCCN 2022037274 | ISBN 9780316412230 (hardcover) | ISBN 9780316421157 (ebook)
Subjects: CYAC: Mystery and detective stories. | Poisoning—Fiction. | Apartment houses—Fiction. | Criminal investigation—Fiction. | LCGFT: Detective and mystery fiction. | Novels.
Classification: LCC PZ7.P27653 Min 2023 | DDC [Fic]—dc23
LC record available at https://lccn.loc.gov/2022037274

ISBNs: 978-0-316-41223-0 (hardcover), 978-0-316-42115-7 (ebook)

Printed in the United States of America

LSC-C

Printing 1, 2023

For Francesca Montoya
—KG

prologue

ADULTS JUST LOVE ASKING US WHAT WE WANT TO BE when we grow up. I guess they think it's cute when we answer, "an astronaut," or "a rock star," or "your boss, so I can make you stop asking me questions."

But it's hard to predict the future. I never even thought about saying I wanted to be a detective, any more than a grass inspector or a night watchman at a mattress store. I don't mean those are bad jobs, or that they aren't interesting in their own ways—they're just jobs I never even thought about.

But that was before the murders in my building. That's right—*murderS*, with a capital *S*. Not one, not two, but...well, keep reading. You'll find out who died, who almost died, and whose lives I helped save.

(Hint: One of them was my own.)

I'm not even the only kid at school who's a detective now. But we don't let just anybody join our club. Our members have to be curious, creative, and good at spotting clues. Does that sound like anyone you know?

Does that sound like...you?

chapter 1

AT THE MARBLE-TOPPED CHESS TABLE IN THE WOOD-paneled lounge of our apartment building, I sat across from my elderly neighbor, Kermit Herman-son. Both of us were playing fast and furiously. I wanted to win so badly it was killing me.

It was my turn, so I moved my knight into the center of the board and stopped my chess clock with a CLICK—starting Kermit's time. We each had only ten minutes to play the whole game.

Kermit raised an eyebrow and stroked his long gray beard. "Are you sure you vant to do zat?" he asked. His accent made him sound like a mad doctor from a monster movie. He's told me he's from

Sweden, and I've never met anyone else from Sweden or whose English sounds like his.

"I've never been so sure of anything in my life," I told him. "Why, are you getting nervous?"

Kermit was hard to beat, so I figured a little trash talking couldn't hurt.

Even though Kermit taught me how to play chess when I was six years old, these days, we rarely played face to face. I usually made my moves on my way to and from school, and he usually made his moves as he came and went from his daily walks around our Chicago neighborhood. But today was Sunday, so when we'd met each other in the elevator, we decided to grab some snacks and sit down for a game.

"Vell, eet ees your funeral," said Kermit, raising one eyebrow.

He smiled and moved his bishop to block me. CLICK.

I had opened with a series of aggressive moves called the Fried Liver Attack. (I know it sounds crazy, but look it up: It's real.) Usually I play defense, because Kermit is a much better player. But this time I wanted to throw him off his game by going on the offense—and his latest move showed me it was actually working.

I attacked again. CLICK.

"I wouldn't call the undertaker yet," I told him.

"You are off to impressive start," admitted Kermit. He had been moving quickly and confidently, but now he was hesitating. "I only hope you know how to checkmate."

"Oh, I know how to checkmate, all right. The only question is how many moves it will take me."

He picked up his queen and then put it back down in the same place. He tugged at his shirt collar like it suddenly felt too tight.

I smelled victory—a victory that would be all the sweeter because I would be there to see the look on his face.

Beads of sweat broke out on Kermit's wrinkly peach-colored forehead. He moved again and stopped his clock again—CLICK—trying to block me with a pawn. But he was only delaying the inevitable. Suddenly, it was like I could see three moves ahead. I knew exactly what I needed to do to steer him toward the endgame.

"Are you sure you want to do that?" I asked, teasing him.

"Maybe not," he admitted. "I am not feelink like myself today."

"Or maybe you've just forgotten what it feels like to lose."

CLICK.

Kermit sipped his tea, which smelled like liquid campfire smoke. He'd already eaten all of his lemon cake except the crumbs.

"Zat ees possible," he said. "Or maybe..."

He frowned.

"Maybe what?" I asked.

It seemed like he was thinking about resigning. In chess, when one player knows they have no way to come back and win, they quit the game by tipping over their queen. It's a super dramatic way to say, *Fine, I give up—you win!*

Well, Kermit gave up, all right. But he didn't tip over his queen.

Instead, he rolled his eyes, knocked the pieces onto the floor—and collapsed onto the chessboard.

chapter 2

"OKAY, VERY FUNNY," I SAID. "YOU DON'T HAVE TO BE so dramatic about losing!"

Kermit didn't move. I glared at him—well, at the wispy gray hair on the top of his head.

"Don't take this the wrong way, but have you considered dandruff shampoo?" I asked.

Still nothing. I was starting to think dandruff might be the least of his problems.

"Kermit?" I asked nervously. "Can you hear me?"

But the chess pieces seemed more likely to answer than he did.

I reached across the board and grabbed Kermit's shoulder. It felt bony and fragile, even through his thick cardigan sweater. I gave him a shake, but not too hard—I didn't want to break anything.

He was limp as a piece of uncooked fish. His back was rising and falling, so at least I knew he was still breathing. Whatever was wrong, there was still time to save him. Unless there wasn't. What if Kermit was dying?

"Help!" I yelled, hoping someone outside the lounge would hear me. "I need help in here!"

No one came.

Stay calm, take deep breaths, and THINK, I told myself. I picked up my phone and called 911.

"What is your emergency?" asked the dispatcher.

"My name is Minerva Keen, and I'm calling from the lobby of the Arcanum on North Dearborn Parkway. My neighbor just collapsed on a chessboard."

"Do you know what happened?"

"Well, he played defense when he should have played offense, but that's probably not what you're asking. My guess is he had a heart attack. He's pretty old."

"An ambulance is on its way," said the dispatcher.

I felt like I should do something to help Kermit, but since his lungs were working, he didn't need CPR. I ran to the front door to tell Oskar, the doorman, to expect an ambulance—and *he* called Delores DeWitt, the building manager.

Moments later, all three of us were standing around poor old Kermit. Oskar looked worried, but Delores stared down at Kermit like he was something gross that needed to be cleaned off the plush Persian rug.

"I've never liked you playing chess down here," she snapped in her gravelly voice.

I wasn't too surprised, because she has never liked me, either. But I snapped right back.

"Are you seriously blaming a board game? That's like saying sitting down is hazardous to your health," I said.

"Maybe it depends on *who* you sit down with," said Delores.

Losing to me couldn't actually have caused Kermit to keel over...could it?

The ambulance came quickly from DuSable Hospital, which is only a few blocks away. My little brother, Heck—I'm twelve, he's eleven—goes there so often that we're on a first-name basis with most of the doctors.

We even knew the EMTs: Joan, who's tiny and has a tattoo of a grinning skull on her arm, and John, who's huge and has a tattoo of a teddy bear. Naturally, we call them Big Joan and Little John. You'd never guess they're fraternal twins.

Big Joan and Little John checked Kermit's vital signs and carefully lifted him onto a gurney. They strapped an oxygen mask over his face and rolled him out to the ambulance while Oskar held the door. Then Big Joan hit the lights and siren and floored it, making the tires smoke and squeal like she was just driving ambulances until she got her big break in NASCAR.

"At least pick up your mess," said Delores, scowling at me as she headed for her office in the back hallway. "And I hope you learned your lesson."

And exactly what lesson was that? I wondered as I replaced the chess pieces on the board.

Everything had happened so fast; one minute, I was playing chess with Kermit, and ten minutes later, I was alone.

Please be okay, I thought, and sank back into my chair with a sick, sad feeling in my stomach.

chapter 3

I PRESSED THE BUTTON AND WATCHED THE ELEVATOR glide down from a higher floor. My building, the Arcanum, is twelve stories tall, 120 years old, and a historical landmark. An atrium in the middle soars all the way up to a huge skylight. Wrought-iron balconies ring the atrium, so I can see my neighbors going in and out of their apartments. It's extremely luxurious but not very private—people are always complaining about the noise when Heck and I play tag.

It's not *our* fault the balconies are perfect for playing tag.

Stepping into the elevator, I pulled the door shut and rode up to our second-floor apartment.

The elevator is like an iron birdcage, so you have to keep your fingers inside while it's moving if you don't want them sliced off.

I needed to talk to Heck about what happened to Kermit, but he was at the farmer's market. And I couldn't talk to our cousin Bizzy, because she was working on her dissertation down at the University of Chicago. And I would have had to wake my parents up if I wanted to talk to them—they were in Australia, where it was still four thirty in the morning.

The Arcanum is like a magnet for people who are different and weird. Lots of famous Chicagoans have lived here over the years, from artists and architects to aldermen and gangsters, and the lawyers who represented the aldermen and gangsters in court.

I guess you could say my family fits right in. My dad, August Keen, is a mathematician specializing in imaginary numbers, and my mom, Aurora Keen, is a philosopher who studies the brain's awareness of itself. Even their casual conversations sound like they're speaking in code. And then there's Heck, who's not only a daredevil but cooks like a professional chef.

If you ask me, I'm pretty normal: I go to school, play AYSO soccer, and once in a while meet up with my neighbor for a game of chess. But if you're the most normal person in a family of circus freaks, you're still kind of a freak, right?

My only problem is that I don't have very many friends, especially since my best friend, Charis, moved to Rancho Cucamonga in California. My mom says other kids are intimidated by my superior brainpower. If that's true, then other kids are looking at it the wrong way, because if I had more friends, my big brain could benefit them, too.

And I also would have had someone to talk to about what just happened in the lobby of the Arcanum.

chapter 4

I DIDN'T HAVE TO WAIT LONG TO TELL THE STORY—BUT it wasn't to anyone I expected.

Forty-five minutes later, I was reading my favorite book (*You're Wrong and I'm Right: How to Win Any Argument, No Matter How Petty*) in my favorite place (lying on the living room couch with pillows under my head and feet) when our buzzer went off. It sounds like a sheep farting through a kazoo.

I closed the book, set it on the living room couch, and walked into our reception hall. Instead of an intercom, we have brass speaking tubes that go all the way down to the lobby. Like I said, the building is 120 years old.

(The tubes are great for pranking people; last year, Heck and I had our neighbors believing that ghosts were whispering to them in the lobby.)

"Who's there, Oskar?" I called down.

"There's a Detective Taylor who says he wants to talk to you, Miss Keen," he told me. His muffled voice sounded like it was coming through the world's longest cardboard tube.

"Send him up," I said.

My mind raced: *Detective? Was he here about Kermit?*

When I opened the door, my mystery guest stared back at me. He had dark brown skin and short salt-and-pepper hair, and he wore a wrinkled blue suit with a tie that looked like ketchup and mustard having a food fight.

"Are you here because of Kermit? Is he okay?"

"Are you Minnie Keen?" he asked.

"It's Mi-ner-va," I said. I refuse to be called Minnie; I'm not miniature and I'm not a mouse.

"I'm Detective Wesley Taylor," he told me. "I'd like to ask you some questions."

I stepped aside to let him in. "That's a coincidence, because I'd like to ask YOU some questions. Like, why are you here?"

He looked at the marble floor, the carved wood panels, and the glittering chandelier in our reception hall like he was recording video with his eyes. Then he took out a notebook and flipped it open.

"I'll go first," said Detective Taylor. "Are your parents home?"

"No. They're in Australia for the next ten weeks as guest lecturers at the University of Melbourne," I told him.

"Do you have a guardian?"

"Bizzy."

"This won't take long, Minerva," said Detective Taylor, sounding annoyed.

"No, that's her name," I told him. "My cousin Elizabetha Burnham goes by Bizzy. She's getting her PhD at the University of Chicago and she's super smart."

"So you're alone?"

"Until Bizzy and my brother, Heck, get back."

"Tell me what happened with Mr. Hermanson this afternoon."

So that *was* why he had come. I told him how Kermit taught me to play when I was little, and how he acted a little bit grumpy but was actually super nice, and even though we usually played chess long-distance, today we'd decided to play in person. I explained how I ran out to the Elegant Grind, the coffee shop on the corner, for my usual order, a half-caf café mocha, and that I got a Russian Caravan tea and a piece of lemon cake for Kermit.

Then I described the game's dramatic ending.

"How did he seem before he collapsed?" asked Detective Taylor.

"He was definitely sweating," I said. "He'd just realized that he'd fallen into my trap."

Detective Taylor raised an eyebrow. "What kind of trap?"

"Not a literal trap—a strategic trap," I said. "And honestly, there are easier ways to get out of losing than going to the hospital. Do you know anything about chess?"

He shook his head. "My game is poker. Did the cake taste in any way unusual?"

"I didn't have any," I told him.

"And why not?"

"It had poppy seeds on it, and they look like bug poop."

"Don't you think it looks suspicious that he collapsed after eating cake you didn't?"

I couldn't believe it. First Delores blamed chess, and now Detective Taylor was blaming a piece of cake like he thought it was poisoned?

Suddenly, I felt so nervous that I burped. I couldn't help it. Some people get dry mouths or wobbly knees or upset stomachs—I burp. Detective Taylor obviously noticed, but fortunately he ignored it.

"You of all people should know that's only circumstantial evidence," I told him, trying to convince him I hadn't done anything wrong. "Just because one event followed another, it doesn't mean they're connected. But are you saying Kermit *didn't* have a heart attack? What's going on?"

Detective Taylor looked at me without any expression. He was probably a great poker player. Then he walked past me and began peering at the oil paintings of my ancestors lining the walls of the reception hall.

"You're very headstrong, Minerva," he said over his shoulder. "Does that ever get you in trouble?"

"Not really," I said, which wasn't a hundred percent true. But it wasn't a lie he could arrest me for, either.

He kept on going into the living room, so I had to follow him. After pulling a few of my parents' books off a shelf and frowning at their bewildering titles (my dad has one called *When N Is Insufficient: The ABCs of X and Y*), he moved on to the corner of our living room, where he stopped. He seemed particularly interested in our glass display case with a collection of vials, flasks, and beakers.

"What can you tell me about these?" he asked.

"They belonged to my great-grandfather, Vitus Keen," I told him. "He was a chemist who made a fortune after he helped invent the timed-release capsule."

Detective Taylor nodded as if the collection of antiques confirmed something he already suspected. I began to wonder what he knew about Kermit—and if talking to Detective Taylor had been a bad idea.

"We'll be seeing each other again very soon, Miss Keen," he said.

chapter 5

I HAD JUST CLOSED THE DOOR BEHIND DETECTIVE TAY-lor when I heard a thud, a yelp, and the sound of falling vegetables.

I yanked the door open again. The detective was sprawled on top of Heck, whose Onewheel was spinning on its side. They were surrounded by tomatoes, broccolini, garlic bulbs, and red onions.

In addition to being an excellent cook who shops at our local farmer's market, Heck is a disaster on anything with wheels—which is why I know what falling vegetables sound like.

I rushed to help Detective Taylor, but he was already climbing to his feet and checking to make sure Heck was okay. Heck bounced right up, as usual.

"Sorry!" said Heck. "I didn't expect anyone to be getting on the elevator."

Detective Taylor helped us pick up the produce and put it back into Heck's shopping bags. "So who's the cook? Your cousin Bizzy?"

My brother and I laughed. Bizzy is smart enough to solve global warming, but she couldn't boil water to save her life.

"I want to be a gourmet chef with my own restaurant," Heck told him.

"He'll do it, too, because everything he makes is to die for," I added—which probably wasn't the best thing to say in front of a suspicious detective.

"Is Heck short for something?" asked Detective Taylor.

Heck nodded.

"His real name is Hector, but he hates that as much as I hate *Minnie*," I explained, wishing I'd had time to talk to my brother before the detective started snooping around.

"And where have you been, Heck?" asked Detective Taylor, taking out his notebook again.

"I've been at the farmer's market since the sun came up," said Heck, lifting one of the bags. "I help out at some of the stalls and they give me free veggies."

Detective Taylor wrote something down, nodded at both of us, and got into the elevator.

I held our apartment door for Heck, who climbed back on his Onewheel and rolled through, using his bags for balance.

"So, what was that all about?" he asked.

I told him everything that happened while he was at the farmer's market. It must have sounded pretty bad, because Heck actually tried to give me a hug.

"What are you doing?" I asked, taking a step back.

"Trying to make you feel better, dummy," he said. "But I still don't understand why that cop was here."

"He's not a cop, he's a police detective," I told him, swallowing another nervous burp. "He wants my help on the case."

"Yeah, and Gordon Ramsay just called and asked me to cohost *MasterChef Junior*," scoffed Heck.

"He might not know he wants my help yet," I admitted. "But he'll figure it out."

Heck rolled his eyes and then rolled into the kitchen to start dinner. I headed for the living room to put on my headphones; when he cooks, it sounds like metal robots fighting with trash-can lids.

What happened to Kermit? I wondered as I flopped back down on the couch. I hoped he was okay. He may have been old enough to be my grandpa, or maybe even my great-grandpa, but he was still my friend.

And if someone had hurt him, I needed to know who it was. Not only to clear my name—but to make sure they couldn't finish the job.

chapter 6

First, I had to find out more about Detective Taylor. It's not every day an actual detective comes knocking on your door—assuming he *was* an actual detective. I burped again. Should I have let him in? It's hard to believe, but there are people who pretend to be police officers. Some of them just think it's fun to bust people for speeding. But there are others who do things a lot worse than that.

And when you think about it, playing a cop is the perfect disguise for a criminal, right?

With my noise-canceling headphones clamped on my head so I couldn't hear Heck, I put on the music I usually use for studying. Then I settled into the couch and opened my laptop. I entered *Detective Wesley Taylor Chicago* into Google search.

Right away I knew he was who he said. The images that popped up looked exactly like the man who had been in my apartment minutes ago. They showed me that he owned a lot more ugly ties, too.

The very first search result was a *Chicago Reader* headline: "Street Cleaner: A Cop Catches a Killer—by Returning to His Past."

I clicked and started reading.

Chicago police detective Wesley Taylor knew something was wrong as he examined the crime scene not far from Montrose Beach. A dog walker had discovered the body of a man not far from a large homeless encampment under Lake Shore Drive.

The first officer on the scene thought the man had frozen to death.

But as Taylor identified the telltale signs of a struggle, he knew he was looking at something even worse.

He was looking at a murder.

After that, I forgot I was reading. The story was written so well, it was more like I was *seeing* it—like there was a movie playing in my head. (The creepy music in my headphones helped. I probably shouldn't study to horror-film soundtracks.)

Detective Taylor had worked on a lot of murder cases. But this one really got to him—because when he was a kid, he had been homeless, too. When he lived in a car with his mom, he couldn't even shower before he went to school. And even though they eventually found a permanent place to live again, Detective Taylor promised himself he would never ignore the homeless people he saw.

After studying case files, Detective Taylor saw a suspicious pattern in the deaths of some homeless people. He became convinced they were all victims of a psychopath. But there were too many homeless people in too many places—and his boss wouldn't assign any other detectives to help him.

So Detective Taylor had gone undercover, even though Chicago's winter was so cold Lake Michigan looked more like the icy Arctic Ocean. He dressed in clothes from the Salvation Army, slept in a flimsy old tent, and spent time getting to know the real homeless men and women who stayed close to where other victims had been found.

He almost became a victim himself. One night, while he was shivering in his sleeping bag, he saw a shadow on the wall of his tent—a large man was ready to swing a heavy iron bar down on Detective Taylor's head!

It's the only time I ever shot another human being in the line of duty, he told the reporter. *But I'm glad I didn't kill him. I want him to spend the rest of his miserable life trapped in that tiny cell, haunted by the faces of his victims.*

I shivered as I finally looked up from my screen.

Detective Taylor wasn't just a poker-faced guy who wore ugly ties—he was a real-life hero. And behind those terrible ties beat a kind and caring heart.

But he was also tough as nails. And he was no quitter. I could tell he would never, ever give up on a case. Now I needed to convince him that we were both on the same side.

chapter 7

BIZZY CAME HOME JUST BEFORE DINNER. WHEN MY brilliant cousin comes into a room, it feels like the wind has blown the door open and everything is flying around.

"Wow, dinner smells fantastic!" she called out as she emptied the contents of her backpack onto an overstuffed chair.

"I know!" answered Heck from the kitchen.

"How was your day?" I asked, closing my laptop and looking up from the couch.

"Highly productive," said Bizzy. "My advisor and I finally settled on a title for my dissertation: 'If Parallel Worlds Exist, Which One Am I In?' But now my head hurts and my feet are actually a little bit sore, too."

I looked down. Her toes were dirty. Probably because she wasn't wearing socks or shoes.

"I think you lost something," I told her.

She followed my eyes, wiggled her toes, and gasped. "Oh! That's so strange! I *know* I was wearing shoes this morning, because I remember taking them off to shake out some gravel."

"You obviously forgot to put them back on," I said. "I'll fill the bathtub so you can wash your feet."

"Thanks, Minerva, I don't know what I'd do without you," said Bizzy, kissing the top of my head and making me squirm.

I'm sure that when my mom asked her big sister, Arabella, if her oldest daughter could look after us while my parents were in Australia, they thought Bizzy would be perfect. After all, she's twenty-five years old and has the biggest brain in our family.

But Bizzy's head is so high up in the clouds that she literally forgets her feet are attached to her body. And the approaching deadline to defend her dissertation had made her even more distracted than usual—leaving me to babysit our babysitter.

Dinner was delicious as always. I told Bizzy all about Kermit while we ate, and she and Heck asked a ton of questions. Both of them thought the whole situation was just as sad and strange as I did. And they were both impressed with Detective Taylor, too.

Since Heck did the cooking, and Bizzy breaks too many glasses, I cleaned up afterward. I scraped food off plates, put leftovers in the fridge, and loaded the dishwasher. I didn't mind that stuff, but when I dumped the trash bag down the garbage chute outside our back door, I opened and closed the hatch as quickly as I could. Unfortunately, I could still hear the bag slide down the chute and slam into one of the big dumpsters in the basement.

Thinking about the basement totally creeps me out. Oskar told me he saw a rat down there—and I *hate* rats (also bats, bugs, spiders, and anything that slithers or wiggles or crawls). Ever since then, I've pictured a family of rats waiting hungrily to make our garbage their dinner, all of them getting big and fat and strong from Heck's cooking.

Gross.

◇◇◇

At bedtime, Heck and I talked though the air vent that connects our bedrooms, something we've done ever since we were old enough to have rooms of our own.

"Why would the police be investigating a case that is most logically a stroke or a heart attack?" I asked my brother while I fluffed the pillow on my queen-sized canopy bed. "Kermit is too nice to have enemies."

"I know you think you know everything," said Heck sleepily. "But as hard as it is for you to believe, they must know something you don't."

"That's what's so frustrating—I want to know it, too," I said.

He yawned so wide I heard his jaw crack. "Well, think it through, Minerva. Either they think they know *what* happened, or they think there's a *reason* for it."

Heck is always most annoying when he's right.

"That gives me an idea," I told him. "Want to know what it is?"

But Heck didn't answer. He'd already fallen asleep.

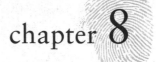

chapter 8

AS SOON AS THE FINAL BELL RANG AFTER SCHOOL, I hurried upstairs to room 203 and dragged all the desks into a big circle. I was still worried about Kermit, but I also had a reason to be excited. It was the third Monday of the new school year, which could mean only one thing.

Club Day.

I had arrived at school half an hour early that morning to hang posters for the new club I was starting: Debate Club. Most people don't know that you don't have to wait until you're angry to have a good argument—you can also do it for fun.

Before school, I had pinned posters on the bulletin board by the water fountain, taped them to the front doors of the school, and even wedged a few into the frames of the mirrors in the girls' bathrooms. There was no way anyone arriving at Jane Byrne Middle School could possibly miss the fact that the Debate Club tryouts would be held at 3:20 p.m. in room 203.

As the minute hand ticked onto the starting time, I opened my notebook and wrote *Debate Club* at the top of a blank page. On the next line, I wrote *Members*. Below that, I wrote, *Minerva Keen, President and Founder.*

I use college-ruled notebook paper, so I still had enough lines for thirty-one more members, and I could always turn over the page if my club was as popular as I hoped it would be.

The hall outside the room began to fill up with kids looking for new groups to join—each room on the second floor had a different club. There was a gaming club, an anime club, a coding club, a book club, a kickball club, and even a club for people who liked to join clubs.

But who doesn't like a good argument?

I saw kids talking and laughing while they walked past, but none of them came into room 203, even though the door was plastered with posters for Debate Club.

Were they afraid they would lose every debate due to my superior brainpower?

The hallway slowly emptied until I couldn't hear any more sneakers squeaking on its polished floor. It was 3:30.

I waited five more minutes, just to be sure, then closed my notebook and stood up with a sigh. A debate club with only one member would never work. People look at you funny if you talk to yourself—if you *argue* with yourself, they cross to the other side of the street.

Were other kids not interested in my club—or were they not interested in me? And if not, why not?

Well, Minerva, I said to myself, *your mom has always said other kids are intimidated by your superior brainpower.*

But who wouldn't want to hang out with a brilliant person who loves to argue? I answered myself.

Uh-oh, I thought. I was doing it: arguing with myself. At least I wasn't doing it out loud.

Suddenly, a kid hurried through the door and sat down in the first desk he saw.

I had my first member!

And he was the last one I would have ever expected.

chapter 9

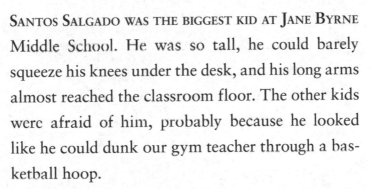

SANTOS SALGADO WAS THE BIGGEST KID AT JANE BYRNE Middle School. He was so tall, he could barely squeeze his knees under the desk, and his long arms almost reached the classroom floor. The other kids were afraid of him, probably because he looked like he could dunk our gym teacher through a basketball hoop.

And even though Santos was just a sixth-grader like me, he was already growing a fuzzy mustache.

"Welcome to Debate Club!" I said.

Santos looked at me like he was trying to decide if I was animal, vegetable, or mineral.

I forgot to mention that, in addition to being the biggest kid at our school, he's also the quietest.

People call him "Silent Santos"—which made me even more surprised that he was interested in Debate Club.

But who knew? Maybe he just wanted to get better at public speaking. With a little encouragement, I bet I could get him to open up.

And it wasn't like anyone else was in line behind him.

I clapped my hands, which seemed to startle him, then stepped inside the circle of desks so I could walk while I talked. It's easier to keep people's attention when you're moving.

"The *Merriam-Webster* dictionary defines 'debate' as 'a regulated discussion of a proposition between two matched sides,'" I told him. "But that doesn't sound very fun, so I define debate as 'an argument.' Do you like to argue?"

From the puzzled expression on his face, I think he had decided to classify me as *vegetable*.

But do vegetables sweat? I was starting to sweat a little. Working with Santos was definitely going to be a challenge.

"I believe I'm qualified to lead this club because I learned logic and argumentation theory from my parents," I told him, plowing ahead. "There may only be two of us, but if we start now and recruit a lot more students, by the time we're in eighth grade, Jane Byrne Middle School can have one of the best debate teams in Illinois!"

Silent Santos dug in his ear, looked at his finger, and then wiped it on the bottom of his seat.

I clapped my hands again and he practically jumped. He would have fallen out of his desk if he wasn't wedged in so tightly.

"For practice, I'll say something and then you'll argue the opposite opinion," I told him. "Ready? Here we go: People learn best when they're sitting down at their desks."

Silent Santos looked at me for almost a minute before finally, slowly, opening his mouth.

He was going to speak!

Then he closed his mouth again.

He popped out of his desk like a champagne cork and started walking away.

"Aha! You're making a point about arguing without words," I said. "Showing that we can learn when we're *not* sitting in our desks."

Then I realized he was actually leaving.

"Wait—where are you going?" I asked, while my heart sank like a key in a toilet.

Finally, Silent Santos said something.

"I'm in the wrong room," he told me.

chapter  10

FIRST MY CHESS PARTNER ENDED UP IN THE HOSPITAL, and now nobody wanted to join my club. It was probably because they were all afraid of debating me, but that still didn't make me feel any better.

Fortunately, when I got home, the whole apartment smelled like I had died and gone to heaven—and heaven was a restaurant that only served breakfast. Heck was making breakfast for dinner again! I followed my nose to the kitchen and found him cooking away. Eggs and bacon were sizzling on the stove...and pancakes were lying all over the floor.

"Why are there pancakes on the floor?" I asked.

"I'm trying to flip them with the pan," he said. "I'm getting really close."

"I'm pretty sure people only do that in cartoons," I told him. "Like making pizza dough by spinning it around and throwing it in the air."

Heck greased a frying pan and heated it on the stove, ready to try again.

"You're wrong," he said. "People really do toss pizza dough in the air. And they flip pancakes with the pan, too."

I know a lot about a lot of things, but I don't cook, so I pulled up a couple of YouTube videos to check. Heck was actually right.

"I'm definitely going to nail it this time," said Heck, pouring some pancake batter into his hot pan.

Looking up, I saw three pancakes sticking to the ceiling.

"It's too bad we can't eat off the floor and the ceiling," I said.

Heck picked up the pan, swirled it to loosen the pancake, and swung it like a tennis player returning a really high shot. The pancake flew into the air...flipped over...and landed on the side that had already cooked.

"You need a one-eighty flip, not a three-sixty," I told him.

"No duh," said my brother.

He tried again, concentrating so hard that his tongue stuck out. This time the pancake flipped perfectly—but Heck had accidentally sent the pan flying. The pancake landed on the floor. The pan clanged off the wall and fell on the handle of the bacon pan, sloshing grease onto the stove top.

Before we could blink, our six-burner stove was a raging bonfire. Crackling red and yellow flames were seconds away from setting our entire kitchen on fire!

I frantically searched for a fire extinguisher, but I didn't find one in the fridge, the freezer, or the recycling bin. (It's hard to think logically when you're afraid of getting fried to a crisp.) I had to figure something out fast—if our apartment caught fire, the whole building could become a towering inferno.

Heck turned off all the burners. Then he hoisted his giant bowl of pancake batter and poured it on top of the fire! The batter sizzled, bubbled, and oozed over the sides of the stove. For a minute, I thought the batter was going to burst into flame, too.

But like a miracle, the fire went out—and stayed out.

We sat down on the floor, staring up at the charred stove top.

"It's not every day someone flips a pancake and destroys a whole stove," I said.

"I was so close to nailing it!" said Heck.

The stove top was so hot that the batter quickly cooked and hardened. Heck cut off a slice, took a bite, and chewed it thoughtfully.

"That's not half bad. I'm going to call this recipe...Stove Top Surprise."

"Forget having your own restaurant. You should have your own TV show," I said. "You could call it *Extreme Cooking Disasters*."

Heck shrugged. "Well, anyway, dinner's ready."

chapter 11

Bizzy came out of her room and joined us at the dining room table. For a few minutes, the only sounds were chewing, swallowing, and whistling as my cousin breathed through her nose. Heck's "Stove Top Surprise" wasn't the best thing he'd ever cooked, but it wasn't the worst, either. (Sometimes I think I can still taste his anchovy omelet.)

While we were eating, I opened my laptop and got to work researching Kermit Hermanson. Heck was right: A detective would only have been assigned to the case if the police suspected foul play. Either they knew Kermit had been poisoned… or they knew there was a reason someone wanted to poison Kermit.

But why would anyone go after an old man whose hobbies were playing chess, taking walks, and sitting on park benches?

I started with a simple Google search, putting his name inside quotation marks, like I was doing a class assignment. There was only one page of results. Apparently, he had complained to Fred Frizzell, the president of our building's co-op board, about icy sidewalks for the past few winters. I couldn't see that being a motive for murder.

Bizzy wiped her mouth with a napkin and glanced at my screen. "Are you researching Kermit?"

I nodded. "He never talks about himself, so I'm trying to find out if someone has something against him. But there's nothing on Google."

"Try the Chicago Public Library's newspaper database," she suggested. "That way you can see if he's ever committed a major crime, been a victim of one, or gotten involved in some controversy."

Logging on to their website with my library card number, I followed Bizzy's instructions and searched. All I found were a few mentions of Kermit competing in amateur chess tournaments.

"Maybe you should check Cook County records," said Bizzy. "Because—whoops!"

The *whoops* was because Bizzy had missed her cup and poured bitter black coffee all over her Stove Top Surprise.

Heck asked for a bite, just to see if coffee somehow improved the taste, but the look on his face told me it didn't.

I took pity on Bizzy and gave her the rest of mine. I didn't really want it, anyway, because it was starting to taste like charred bacon grease.

Then I opened a new browser tab to search public records. The very first result made me gasp.

"What is it?" asked Heck.

"A legal record of a name change. Kermit Hermanson used to be called Kermit Herascov."

"See? You just need to know where to look. Now you need to find out why he changed his name," said Bizzy, like it was no big deal and she learned about people's secret identities all the time.

I Googled *Kermit Herascov* and found dozens of pages of results. Kermit wasn't Swedish—he was Russian. And not just any Russian, either. After leading protests against the dictatorial president of the Russian Federation, he'd been forced to flee to the U.S.

Because the Russian secret police had tried to kill him.

With poison.

"Maybe you should make files to keep track of all this information," suggested Bizzy.

"*Case* files," I said. "Good idea."

"What's that sound?" asked Heck.

I could faintly hear tapping from the other side of the apartment.

The front door! I pushed back my chair and raced out of the dining room, through the living room, and into the entry hall.

I looked through the peephole and recognized the curly-haired woman on the other side. I didn't know her name, but she was a building neighbor I'd seen around for years, usually while she was waiting for her nervous chihuahua to poop on the sidewalk. She looked incredibly sad.

I opened the door.

"I'm so, so, so sorry your friend Kermit died!" she said, bursting into tears.

CASE FILES

Name: Kermit Hermanson AKA
Kermit Herascov

Occupation: Political activist
(retired)

Relationship to case: First poisoning victim

Hair: White, thin on top, bad case of dandruff

Eyes: Crinkly, watery

Age: Old (like great-grandfather old)

Identifying characteristics: Bushy white beard
(perfect for hiding things under)

Personality: Nice...but mysterious

Habits, behavior & special talents: Good at chess
(even good enough to beat ME!)

DETECTIVE'S NOTES:

It's hard to believe a guy whose hobbies are taking
walks and sitting on park benches led an
uprising against the evil president of
Russia!

It's even harder to believe the president of Russia had him POISONED. Thankfully, Kermit survived.

But how bad is his luck to get poisoned AGAIN?

I thought Kermit was just a nice old guy who liked to play chess and eat cake, but it turns out he had a lot of secrets.

(The Arcanum has a lot of secrets, too.)

I didn't think I had much more to learn about chess, but he definitely taught me a thing or two.

I just hope he stays alive long enough for me to show him exactly how much I've learned....

chapter 12

"KERMIT'S *DEAD*? ARE YOU SURE?" I ASKED.

Her bad news made me feel like the floor had disappeared from under me and I was falling down a deep, dark hole.

"I heard it from my neighbor, who heard it from Delores DeWitt," said the curly-haired woman, wiping tears away with her sleeve. "I know you played chess together. Please accept my condolences— I just feel so terrible for you!"

Heck had arrived in time to hear what she was saying. She looked at the two of us and then began backing away.

"I'm sure you're very busy, so I won't take any more of your time," she said. "Besides, I need to tell Kermit's other friends how terrible I feel for them, too. It's all just so terribly *tragic!*"

"We have to go to the hospital," I told Heck as soon as I closed the door.

"Shouldn't we just wait for the funeral?" he asked.

Now I was crying, too. "There might not be one. Kermit doesn't have any family. I want to say goodbye while I still have the chance."

Heck was going to ride his bike, Onewheel, scooter, or skateboard to the hospital, but I already had enough to worry about without him crashing. So I made him walk with me.

When we got there, I bought a bouquet of flowers in the gift shop. The fact that Kermit wouldn't be able to see or smell them almost made me start crying again.

"Oh, hi, Heck," said the receptionist. "Are you checking in?"

Heck has been to the ER as a patient so many times they should give him frequent-crasher miles.

"He's fine," I told her. "We're here to say good-bye to our neighbor, Kermit Herascov—I mean, Hermanson."

She tapped on her keyboard, frowned at her screen, then looked up.

"He won't be going anywhere for a while. He's still unconscious."

At first, I didn't think I heard her correctly. The words didn't make sense.

"Wait—he's alive?" I asked, confused.

The receptionist smiled. "He's in critical condition, but I wouldn't give up hope just yet."

Suddenly, I didn't feel like I was falling down a deep, dark hole anymore. I felt like a net had caught me just before I went splat on the bottom— and launched me upward again.

"Can we see him?" I asked hopefully.

"You'll have to check with his nurse."

Heck and I hurried to the elevator as I wondered why Delores DeWitt would have told someone Kermit was dead. Maybe it was a misunderstanding... or maybe it was wishful thinking.

On Kermit's floor, Nurse Rosamie looked surprised to see Heck walking on his own two feet.

"What's wrong this time?" she asked him.

"He's *fine*," I told her, feeling annoyed that everyone kept wanting to help my brother. "We're here to see our neighbor, Kermit Hermanson."

"Well, the old man gave us quite a scare yesterday and we're not out of the woods yet," said Nurse Rosamie. "His vitals are unstable and he's still unconscious."

She led us to his room. Kermit had an oxygen tube under his nose, an IV in his arm, and so many wires attached to his body that he looked like a marionette with no one to pull his strings. Only the slow rise and fall of his chest and the beeping of his heart monitor told us he was still alive.

"Have they figured out what's wrong with him?" I asked as I put the flowers on the windowsill.

Nurse Rosamie shook her head. "The doctors won't tell me, but I've seen them talking to the police."

I looked at Kermit's kind face and tangled beard. He sure didn't look like someone who could make a dictator feel threatened.

"Is there a chessboard in this hospital?" I asked.

Heck rolled his eyes. "Don't you ever think about anything else, Minerva? I'm not playing with you—and he definitely can't."

"Actually, we do have a games closet to keep the patients from getting bored," Nurse Rosamie told me.

"Speaking of games…" said Heck, leaving the room without finishing his sentence.

After Rosamie dropped off the chess game, I unfolded the board on the table next to Kermit's bed. I set up all the pieces and made an opening move with a white pawn.

When Kermit woke up, I wanted him to know I'd been there.

If he woke up.

I was just leaving when Detective Taylor appeared in the doorway. He was wearing the same wrinkled blue suit, but today's tie reminded me of strawberries dissolving in lime Jell-O.

"Why are you here?" he asked suspiciously.

"Because he's my friend," I told him. "And apparently, he has a powerful enemy who wants him dead."

Detective Taylor narrowed his eyes. "An enemy with access to exotic toxins—possibly delivered in a timed-release capsule. Would you know anything about that?"

chapter 13

DETECTIVE TAYLOR AND I STEPPED INTO THE HALL. IT seemed rude to talk about assassination attempts in Kermit's presence. On the other side of the nurse's station, Heck had hijacked a wheelchair and was trying to pop a wheelie.

"I'm not *Russian*, if that's what you mean," I told Detective Taylor.

"Why would you think I think you're Russian?" he asked, like he didn't know what I was talking about.

"Well, you can't still think I poisoned Kermit, because that's ridiculous."

"Who said anything about poison?"

"You did."

The detective's poker face finally broke and he looked frustrated with himself as he realized I was right. Maybe he was human, after all.

I had noticed three things about Detective Taylor. One, he spoke mostly in questions. Two, if I didn't answer right away, he just kept waiting, which made me feel more pressure to say something. Three, he tried hard not to let me know what he was thinking.

I would have written down my observations, but I didn't have a notebook.

Oh yeah—four, he always carried a notebook.

"Look, you and I both know that Kermit Hermanson is really Kermit Herascov," I told Detective Taylor. "We also both know that a certain evil someone in Russia wants him dead. So you can't really suspect me. What I'm wondering is, why isn't this a case for the FBI?"

"How do you know the FBI *isn't* involved?" he asked.

He even answered questions with questions!

I decided to fight fire with fire: "Well, *are* they?"

At the far end of the hall, Heck was working up speed in the wheelchair. It looked like he was trying to go around the corner on one wheel.

"Minerva, do you really think I would reveal such important information to a potential suspect in a crime?" asked Detective Taylor.

"You haven't answered any other questions, so I don't know why you'd start now. You only speak in questions, don't you?"

He *almost* smiled. "What do you think?"

"I think I can help you," I told him. "After all, we both want to know the same thing: who tried to kill Kermit. I can be your eyes and ears at the Arcanum—your assistant detective. People will talk to me because I'm just a kid."

Detective Taylor smoothed his ugly tie. He tapped his pen on his notepad. He seemed to be considering my offer. Or maybe he was considering whether I was still a suspect. But before he could say anything, there was a crash at the end of the hall, followed by the sound of falling bedpans.

Guess how I know what falling bedpans sound like.

"Don't you think you'd better go check on your brother?" asked Detective Taylor.

"Do *you* think I should go check on my brother?"

Then I heard nurses and doctors shouting and I knew the answer.

"Think about it!" I called as I jogged off toward the scene of Heck's latest accident. "Maybe we could solve this case together!"

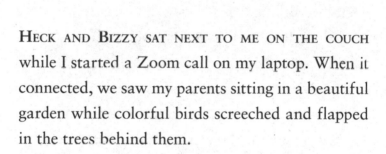

HECK AND BIZZY SAT NEXT TO ME ON THE COUCH while I started a Zoom call on my laptop. When it connected, we saw my parents sitting in a beautiful garden while colorful birds screeched and flapped in the trees behind them.

They were wearing light jackets, because even though it was warm early fall in Chicago, it was chilly spring in Melbourne. Plus, it was daytime there and nighttime here—when you're on opposite sides of the world, everything is completely backward. Their work takes them away a lot. Before Australia, they spent three months in Vancouver, Canada, and next year they're headed off to Birmingham, England.

"Check this out!" said Heck proudly, showing them the cast on his left arm. "I crashed a wheelchair at the hospital."

"You had an accident *at* the hospital?" asked Dad, not sounding very surprised.

"Minerva was playing chess with Kermit Hermanson, that old guy from the building, when he keeled over and practically died," said Bizzy. "They went to visit him."

"How long will you have to wear the cast, Heck?" asked Mom.

"Only a couple of weeks—it's a soft cast because I just sprained my wrist," Heck explained.

"Don't worry about me," I said, wondering if I'd have to break both arms to get their attention. "I only watched a friend almost die."

Mom and Dad looked like they wished they could change the subject. They're more comfortable with big ideas than big emotions.

"Is Kermit all right?" Mom finally asked.

"No!" I told her. "He's unconscious. The police think he was poisoned, and I have a theory about how it happened."

"Let me guess: You're going to tell us," said Dad.

"Kermit seemed fine when we met in the elevator and decided to play," I said while I still had everyone's attention. "Then I ran out to the Elegant Grind and brought back my coffee, plus tea and cake for Kermit. He collapsed right after he polished off the cake."

"You should have had *me* make the cake," said Heck, sticking a finger under his cast to scratch an itch.

"Anyway, Bizzy's suggestion led me to discover that Kermit's real last name is Herascov and he's Russian—and not just any Russian, but someone they've tried to silence before," I continued. "I think there was a Russian assassin working undercover at the Elegant Grind, just waiting for a chance to poison Kermit's food."

Dad looked dubious. "But if *you* placed the order, how would they have known it was for *him*?"

I tried to remember if I had told anyone at the coffee shop that the tea and cake were for Kermit. Even if I hadn't, it was possible they had spied on him long enough to know I was his regular chess partner.

"Maybe they knew Kermit drinks that particular kind of tea?" suggested Bizzy helpfully.

"I just don't think it adds up," said Dad, shaking his head.

Mom said they had to get dressed for a cocktail party, so they logged off. I was mad at both of them for not caring more, and even madder at Dad for poking holes in my theory. Maybe I was wrong about the little details, but I knew I was right about the big picture.

No one believed me. How could I convince them?

chapter 15

I WAS STARING AT THE SIDEWALK WHILE I TRUDGED home after school on Tuesday, so I almost didn't notice the ambulance idling in front of the Arcanum. When I saw its flashing red lights shining on the toes of my sneakers, I finally looked up.

Oskar was holding the door for Big Joan and Little John, the EMTs, who were guiding a gurney out onto the sidewalk. They weren't hurrying at all, which was strange, since there was somebody on the gurney.

Then I realized why they were moving so slowly: Their patient was covered in a sheet.

The *somebody* was a *body*.

I started running, thinking, *Please don't let it be...*

Please don't let it be *who*? I didn't know how to finish the sentence. I didn't want it to be *anybody*, but I especially didn't want it to be anyone I knew.

The ambulance burned rubber and roared away before I was halfway down the block—Big Joan was still practicing for her NASCAR tryout. And by the time Oskar opened the front door to let me in, I was panting so hard that I could barely speak.

"Who...was...that?" I asked him.

"Serenity Meadows," Oskar told me sadly. "From 1102."

"Is she really...?"

Oskar nodded. "She collapsed getting into the elevator on the eleventh floor. By the time it reached the lobby she was gone."

I remembered who Serenity was because she had an unusual name like me. She was pretty and always accessorized her workout clothes with flowers and crystal jewelry. Young and healthy looking, she was the exact opposite of Kermit.

But if she had suddenly collapsed just like he did, maybe there was a connection between them. Had she stood up to the Russian dictator, too? Had she also changed her name? Was she secretly working with Kermit, who lived on the floor above her?

I hurried through the lobby, crossed the atrium, and opened the door to the manager's office. Delores DeWitt was looking at eBay, like one of her residents hadn't just dropped dead.

"I need to see Serenity Meadows's apartment," I told her. "I think I might know who had her killed."

Delores made a dry, rasping sound, like she had a leaf caught in her throat. I think she was trying to laugh.

"So you're a detective now," she said, her voice dripping with sarcasm. "What makes you think I would let you trespass in a private residence? And what makes you think there was even a crime?"

"I'm sure Detective Taylor thinks so," I told her.

"Then talk to him," said Delores. "But don't ask me to give you a good character reference—I might have to show him my file."

She pulled a fat folder off a nearby shelf, dropped it on her desk, and petted it like she thought it might start purring. It was labeled KEEN KIDS and I knew what was inside: copies of all the reports she sent to our parents every time she caught us doing anything she didn't like. The longest one (ten pages) was about a complete accident. Someone had been stealing our newspaper every morning, and all we did was hide a glue-and-glitter bomb under it to catch them. Unfortunately, a janitor accidentally pushed it with his broom, and both the janitor and the atrium were covered in glitter that wouldn't wash off for a week.

Delores hates kids. But she seems to hate me and Heck in particular.

"Don't worry," I told her, getting ready to slam the door on my way out. "I wouldn't count on you for a character reference if my life depended on it."

Then I remembered I had a question.

"Why did you tell someone Kermit was dead?" I asked.

Delores shrugged and put the folder back on

her shelf. "I said it *looked like* he'd dropped dead. You know how rumors spread."

I slammed the door, thinking, *I hope YOU drop dead!*

In the elevator, I stared at the buttons for a minute. Then, instead of pressing 2, I pressed 11. I watched the atrium floor grow smaller and smaller below me as the elevator climbed almost to the top of the building. Was it always so loud? The ancient metal contraption sounded badly in need of oil as it squeaked and screeched its way upward.

I thought I felt a hiccup coming but no, it was a nervous burp—kind of a hic-burp. Sneaking into Serenity's apartment seemed crazy, but if I could find anything that connected her with Kermit, I knew I could help Detective Taylor break the case.

On the eleventh floor, I tiptoed along the balcony, staying close to the wall so the people on lower floors couldn't see me. I put my ear to the door of apartment 1102 and listened. It was completely silent inside.

The doorknob turned, but the door didn't open. The deadbolt was locked.

I looked up. All the apartments in the building have transoms, little rectangular windows above the front doors that residents sometimes leave open for better ventilation. But Serenity's was closed.

I headed back to the elevator. There was still one more thing I could try.

On the second floor, I went through our apartment, out the back door, and past the garbage chute to the fire stairs. People don't always lock their back doors because the stairs are inside the building and there's a security door at the bottom.

Nine flights of stairs was a lot more than I usually climb. By the time I reached the eleventh floor again, I was tired, sweaty, and wheezing like a flat-faced dog.

Serenity's back door was unlocked. I gave it a push and it swung open silently.

My nervous burp was *not* silent—it echoed in the small vestibule like the belch of a frightened bullfrog.

It was time to start my search. Taking a deep breath, I opened the inner door and stepped through.

I found myself standing in Serenity's kitchen, which was no surprise. What *was* a surprise was that Detective Taylor was standing in it, too. He was wearing blue rubber gloves and it looked like he had been taking food out of the cupboards.

Only now he was staring at me.

I burped—a long, low, rumbly one—and Detective Taylor wrinkled his nose.

"This isn't what it looks like," I said.

CASE FILES

Name: "Big Joan" Jonker & "Little John" Jonker

Occupation: Emergency Medical Technicians (EMTs)

Relationship to case: Every time someone gets poisoned, they are first to the scene of the crime!

Hair: Fire-engine red (Joan), strawberry blond (John)

Eyes: Forward, watching traffic!

Age: The same, since they're fraternal twins. Maybe 30?

Identifying characteristics: Skull tattoo (Joan), teddy bear tattoo (John). Joan is tiny, like an elf, and John is giant, like a...giant. I have no idea which genius gave them their nicknames.

Personality: Way too nice. (Considering that they have to deal with gross accidents all day long.)

Habits, behavior & special talents: Little John moves kind of slowly but Big Joan more than makes up for him. If she drove a race car and not an ambulance, she'd be racking up the trophies!

DETECTIVE'S NOTES:

If I had a NORMAL family, I would never have gotten to know Big Joan and Little John. But my brother is Hector "Heck" Keen, who never met an accident he couldn't get into.

Starting when he was two (and got all his fingers and toes caught in the baby gate), Heck has been collecting frequent-crasher miles at the hospital. Big Joan and Little John have been his chauffeurs every single time.

Fortunately, they never complain. (My parents actually send them presents on their birthday.) I honestly think they just like helping people...even people like Hazardous Heck!

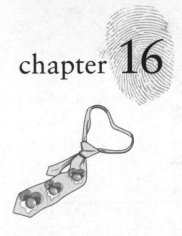

chapter 16

DETECTIVE TAYLOR SET A BAG OF FLOUR ON THE counter and folded his arms.

"Minerva, do you know what we call a person who shows up at two seemingly unrelated crime scenes?" he asked.

"A suspect," I guessed.

"That's right," he said.

"Well, do you know who else shows up at seemingly unrelated crime scenes?" I shot back. "A detective."

"Is that what you think you are?" he asked.

I looked around as I gathered my thoughts. There was flour, sugar, and baking powder on the counter, three key ingredients for baking a cake.

Detective Taylor's latest tie had a broken-egg pattern—all he needed now was milk and butter.

"Yes, I was with Kermit when he collapsed, which was a coincidence," I told him. "But I haven't been home all day. When Serenity collapsed, I was still at school. You can talk to my teachers if you need an alibi."

Detective Taylor sighed. "And what, exactly, were you hoping to accomplish by sneaking in through the back door of this apartment?"

"To help you solve the case! If we can find how Serenity was connected to Kermit, we can prove the attempts on their lives were ordered by the leader of the Russian Federation."

Detective Taylor looked up at all the cabinets he still had left to search. He seemed annoyed, like he was tired of talking and wanted to get back to work.

"And what if there is no connection?" he asked. "What if these are two completely separate incidents?"

"They *have* to be connected," I insisted.

He sighed and tightened his gloves. "If you want to be a detective, start by keeping an open mind.

Let the facts lead you to your conclusions, and not the other way around. Now it's time for you to go."

I headed for the front door, because I didn't want to climb all those stairs again, even going down. A crime-scene squad arrived just as I got there. The two women and one man raised all six of their eyebrows when they saw me, but I just shrugged. I didn't feel like explaining why Detective Taylor had dismissed me—or letting them see what I was going to do next.

I waited until they went into the kitchen, then used the long brass rod by the door to open Serenity's transom from the inside. I slipped out and closed the door behind me.

For a while, I couldn't hear anything, but eventually, Detective Taylor and his team moved close enough that their voices carried through the transom window.

"Get all those food items to the lab for testing ASAP," Detective Taylor said.

"I'm on it," said one of the women. "Do you think there's any connection to the old guy?"

"It depends on the autopsy results," said Taylor. "But I seriously doubt we're going to find the same exotic poison in both victims."

"Yeah, what are the odds of *that*?" said the man.

"We need to find out who saw her last," said Taylor.

"The doorman told me she had several boy-friends," volunteered the other woman.

Boyfriends? I thought. They were getting way off track. Even if one of Serenity's boyfriends had poisoned her, why would he poison Kermit?

I needed to find out how they were connected— and fast.

When I heard the doorknob turning behind me, it caught me completely off guard. I dove into an alcove just as Detective Taylor stepped out onto the balcony.

"Search this apartment from top to bottom," he told his team. "I'm going back to the station to work the phone."

I held my breath until he was gone.

chapter 17

WHEN I GOT BACK TO OUR APARTMENT, HECK WAS making himself an after-school snack of home-made ramen noodles with slices of roast pork and a quail's egg the size of a malted milk ball. His friends had signed his cast but their signatures were already blurry from ramen broth.

After kicking off my shoes, I grabbed a hand-ful of Cheez-Its and sat down at the dining room table, where I opened my laptop to research Seren-ity Meadows.

There were two of them, it turned out. The first one was a cemetery outside Tampa, Florida.

The second one was the woman who lived in my building.

It was hard to believe Serenity's next address would be marked by a tombstone. She looked so alive in the pictures she'd posted on Instagram: doing yoga poses, working out in a gym, playing volleyball on North Avenue Beach, and trying on lots and lots of outfits.

She also took dozens of selfies with guys who were obviously excited to be with her. Maybe they liked shopping, too.

But I still thought Detective Taylor and his team were wasting their time interviewing Serenity's boyfriends.

Heck sat down next to me and started reading over my shoulder while he slurped his noodles, splashing my arm in the process. To get him back, I blew the orange cracker crumbs off my keyboard into his face.

"Oskar told me what happened," he said.

"I was just trying to find her connection to Kermit," I told him.

"How do you know they're connected?"

"They *have* to be. It's super rare to have even one poisoning. What are the chances that two people living in the same building got poisoned for different reasons?"

I clicked on the website for Serenity Now, which was a "holistic gym" close to our building. The "About Us" page listed Serenity Meadows as the founder and owner and also had a short biography of her. It said she had been born and raised in Normal, Illinois, before studying sports medicine at the University of Illinois. Aside from her belief in the healing powers of crystals—which, if you ask me, are about as magical as ordinary rocks—she seemed as normal as the place she grew up.

"She sure doesn't look like an enemy of the Russian Federation," said Heck, still crowding me.

"Neither does Kermit," I reminded him as I shoved him away.

Secretly, I had to admit Heck might be right. Serenity's life story was all over the web, and she had obviously never changed her name. There was also no indication that she even knew where Russia was, much less had an opinion about its cruel leader.

So unless the president of the Russian Federation was an angry ex-boyfriend, there was zero reason he'd target her.

"If she's not connected to Kermit or Russia, that means one of two things," I said, thinking out loud. "Either there are two murderers with different motives, and both of them are using poison... or there's one murderer who has a single motive for murdering two very different people."

Heck sucked up a noodle like an anteater retracting its tongue, flinging a few more drops of broth onto my screen.

"If there's only one murderer, they probably live in our building, close to the scenes of the crimes," he said.

He was right. And since we didn't know the motive, we had no way of knowing if there were more murders to come—and who would be next. What if someone in the building had something against Bizzy...or Heck...or me?

Closing my laptop, I pushed my chair back and slid my feet into my sneakers.

"Where are you going?" Heck asked.

"To the police station," I told him. "I want to talk to Detective Taylor."

Heck's eyes got wide. "You'd better hope he doesn't lock you up while you're there!"

CASE FILES

Name: Serenity Meadows

Occupation: Gym owner

Relationship to case: Second poisoning victim

Hair: Brown, usually in a ponytail with a scrunchie

Eyes: Made up (but beautiful!!)

Age: Who knows? I'm going to guess twenty-six.

Identifying characteristics: Worked out wearing makeup and jewelry. Very fit but didn't sweat.

Personality: Everyone seemed to like her, especially boys.

Habits, behavior & special talents: Loved shopping, and boys, and shopping with boys.
  (Shopping FOR boys???)

BUY SCRUNCHIE!!

DETECTIVE'S NOTES:

Even though health nut Serenity Meadows was a successful entrepreneur who started her own business, she was also just plain nutty.

She thought rocks have magic powers and people give off good or bad vibrations. She also believed in astrology—that the stars and planets can predict what will happen in the future. But she sure didn't see this one coming!

Her website says she ALSO believed in reincarnation—that souls can be reborn in different bodies. I believe in science, not New Age stuff, but for her sake, I hope she's right.

chapter 18

"WHAT CAN I DO FOR YOU, MINERVA?" ASKED DETEC-
tive Taylor.

"I was hoping we could talk in your office," I
told him.

There were a dozen other people waiting in the
lobby of the police station and I didn't want any of
them to overhear what I had to say. The poisoner
could have been anywhere.

Detective Taylor sighed and used an electronic
key to unlock the door behind him. He motioned
for me to follow.

His "office" turned out to be one desk of many
in a large, open room. A few other detectives were
working nearby. A depressed-looking man in a

tuxedo, who was handcuffed to a chair, watched us as we crossed the room.

"Ignore the guy in the tux," said Detective Taylor.

"What did he do?" I asked.

"That's Amazing Andy. He claims to be a birthday-party magician, but the only thing he makes disappear is the birthday presents."

Amazing Andy looked like he wished he could make himself disappear.

As soon as I sat down across from Detective Taylor, I asked, "Have you gotten the lab reports back on the poison yet?"

"Those typically take a few days," he told me.

He was still wearing the same broken-egg-patterned tie—only now it looked like it had actual egg on it, too. Maybe he ate breakfast for dinner when he was hard at work on a case.

"I know I was wrong," I admitted. "Kermit and Serenity couldn't have both been poisoned by Russian agents, because Serenity has no connection to Russia. Which makes this case a whole lot harder."

"It certainly does," agreed Detective Taylor.

"But I still think it's probably one murderer, even if he or she has a different motive for each victim," I continued. "What are the odds that two people in the same building would both be poisoned by *different* people?"

"Pretty long odds," he agreed.

"If it is one person, though, how could the same person hold grudges against both an old chess player *and* a young fitness fanatic?"

"That's the million-dollar question," said Detective Taylor.

"Is the reason you're not telling me anything that you still think I'm a suspect?"

Now *I* was sounding like a detective—speaking only in questions.

He shook his head. "Even supposing a twelve-year-old-girl had poisoned two people, I don't think she'd be pestering the police to solve the case. Besides, your alibi checked out."

That was a relief. But I didn't like being called a pest.

Behind Detective Taylor, Amazing Andy reached inside his jacket with his free arm and removed a black leather wallet. With a slow smile, he opened it to reveal a police badge.

"I think Amazing Andy stole someone's badge," I whispered.

By the time Detective Taylor turned around, the wallet had disappeared. He crossed the room and turned the magician's pockets inside out, finding a bouquet of flowers, a string of silk handkerchiefs, a frightened white mouse—and finally, the pick-pocketed badge.

Amazing Andy winked at me.

"Thanks for spotting that," said Detective Taylor gruffly as he put the badge back in his pocket and sat down. "Listen, the reason I'm not telling you anything isn't because you're a suspect. It's because you're a civilian."

"Would an average civilian have discovered as much as I have?" I asked.

Detective Taylor looked at his watch—maybe he wanted to make sure it was still there. "You're very sharp, Minerva, but you're not exactly ahead of us."

"Maybe it would help if I had a notebook like yours so I could write things down. Can you tell me where to get one?"

He opened a desk drawer and started rummaging inside it. While his head was down, I noticed a scribble on the pad of paper by his desk phone. Reading bad handwriting upside down wasn't easy, but I had just deciphered it when he closed the drawer and looked up again.

I tried not to show any reaction as Detective Taylor slid a pocket-sized notebook across the desk and then handed me a business card.

"My cell phone number is on the back," he said. "If you really want to prove you're cut out for detective work, Minerva, bring me something I don't already know."

The notebook wasn't a badge, obviously, but in a way, I felt like he'd just made me his deputy.

"You won't regret this," I promised.

I felt so proud I thought my heart would

explode, or my head, or both—which would have been a disaster, because then I couldn't have solved anything. But I was already catching up to his investigation. Because this is what he'd scribbled:

Hermanson and Meadows poisons MATCH!!!

chapter  19

IT WAS DARK OUTSIDE WHEN I LEFT THE POLICE STA-
tion. I didn't know the area very well, so I walked
home on the busiest and brightest street, looking
over my shoulder from time to time. In some parts
of Chicago, getting poisoned is the least of your
worries.

I should have felt better when I reached my own
neighborhood, but my mind was playing tricks on
me, and I couldn't stop picturing Serenity's lifeless
body under the sheet on the stretcher. Since the
hospital was only a block out of my way, I decided
to stop by and make sure Kermit hadn't gotten any
worse. But I knew they didn't like nighttime visitors. So instead of checking in, I just breezed past

the reception desk like I had somewhere important to be.

Kermit's eyes were still closed, and if anything, he had even more wires and tubes plugged into him than before. There was a computer on a wheeled stand next to his bed. Hoping to read the doctor's diagnosis, I tapped the space bar to wake it up.

ENTER USER ID AND PASSWORD, it demanded.

I could probably have guessed a user ID from a nurse's name. Could I crack the password?

"No gaming on hospital computers," said a voice behind me.

After I landed—I was so surprised that I actually jumped—I turned around and saw Nurse Rosamie.

"I wasn't trying to play a game," I told her.

"It's after visiting hours anyway," she said with a tired smile.

"Is Kermit doing any better?" I asked hopefully.

Nurse Rosamie crossed the room to his bed. "The good news is that his heartbeat has stabilized. The bad news is that we still haven't seen him regain consciousness. If he doesn't open his eyes soon, he might never wake up."

I watched as she examined the connections on his wires and tubes, checked his fluid levels, and studied the squiggly lines and flashing lights on the monitors. It was almost like she was a mechanic and he was a car—until she gently raised his head to fluff his pillow.

Kermit seemed so helpless that I suddenly worried the murderer might try to sneak in and finish the job.

"Has anyone else come to visit him?" I asked.

Nurse Rosamie shook her head. "As far as I can tell, this old guy is all alone in the world."

"He has me," I reminded her.

"Then he's lucky," she said, smiling again. "I need to finish my rounds. And you should go home. It's getting late."

"I'll leave in just a minute," I promised.

After she left, I sat down on the edge of the bed and held Kermit's hand. It was cold, bony, and badly in need of moisturizer. But I could feel a faint pulse of blood beneath his skin.

"Hang in there, Kermit," I told him.

As I stood up to leave, I glanced at the chessboard I had set up on my previous visit. I didn't realize anything had changed at first. Then I saw it.

A black pawn had been moved out to block my white pawn.

I felt a smile forcing its way onto my face as warmth flooded my entire body.

Kermit had responded to my opening move!

chapter 20

I PRACTICALLY FLOATED TO SCHOOL ON WEDNESDAY. IF Kermit had woken up and felt well enough to move a chess piece, there had to be a chance he'd get better.

There was another surprise waiting when I got to my math class: Silent Santos.

I didn't even know he was *in* my math class. Then again, I sit right in front of the teacher, and he was sitting all the way in the back of the room. He's so quiet that I guess I never noticed him.

I waved at him before I sat down. He didn't wave back.

The bell rang and Mrs. Binomial smiled at us like she was about to announce a pizza party.

I knew that meant bad news. She's as sweet as a grandmother, but when she gives out homework, it's like she thinks she's sending you home with a slice of homemade pie.

"This morning, we're going to see how much you've all learned in the first few weeks of school," she announced.

As she picked up the stack of tests, everyone groaned—except for me and Santos. Tests are no big deal for me. And Santos doesn't talk, so why would he groan?

Mrs. Binomial dropped a test on my desk as she began making her way around the room.

"You have thirty minutes to complete this," she said. "You may not be able to finish, because there are a lot of questions. Just do your best."

I flipped through the test. It was three pages long, and two of those pages were double-sided. Fifty questions! This was going to be a challenge, even for me. Soon the only sound was twenty-seven pencils scribbling.

Make that twenty-six.

Five minutes into the test, I heard footsteps at the back of the room. I craned my neck and saw Santos standing at the window. He was staring at something outside.

"Eyes forward, Minerva," said Mrs. Binomial from her desk. "And Santos, when you're ready, please return to your seat."

Let's just say Santos didn't exactly hurry. A few minutes later, he shuffled back to his desk.

Better get to work, Santos, I thought.

The questions were harder than usual. Our teacher may have claimed this was all review, but I was pretty sure there were things we hadn't covered yet. They weren't hard for me—remember, my dad knows everything there is to know about imaginary numbers—but I couldn't exactly rush through them, either.

After twelve minutes, I heard the sound of crumpling paper and then a KER-THUNK. Santos was on the move again. This time, he was at the back of the classroom, shooting baskets in the trash can.

"Santos, please don't distract the others," said Mrs. Binomial sweetly.

He shrugged and sat down again.

After sixteen minutes, I heard a pencil roll slowly off a desk and bounce on the floor. Santos walked up to the front of the room and dropped his test on the teacher's desk.

He's not even going to bother finishing it!

Santos didn't look down as he walked past me to his desk.

I shook my head and got back to work. I needed to concentrate on my own test if I was going to finish without making any mistakes.

After eighteen minutes, Mrs. Binomial cleared her throat and looked up. She had just finished grading Santos's test.

"One hundred percent as usual, Santos!" she called out. "Very well done. I hope the rest of you will be inspired by Mr. Salgado's shining example."

Wait...what?

Everyone turned around and looked at Santos, surprised, but he glared at them until they stopped.

I hurried through the rest of the test. This new information just didn't compute. Santos was strong and silent...*but he was also smart?*

I was the next one to finish. After twenty-five minutes, I took my test up to Mrs. Binomial and watched her grade it.

"Very good, Minerva," she said when she was finished. "You only missed one!"

One?

Was Silent Santos even smarter than me?

chapter 21

WHEN I SPOTTED SANTOS WALKING DOWN THE HALL after lunch, I didn't even think twice before I ran up behind him and tapped him on the shoulder. I never expected him to be so surprised that he'd drop what he was carrying.

Unfortunately, what he was carrying was a large tray of tiny bean sprouts planted in paper cups. When he dropped it, the cups exploded like dirt bombs while the tray skidded across the floor.

The kids around us gasped and stepped back. I think they expected Silent Santos to pick me up by the feet and plant me upside down in a trash can.

Before he could attack, I dropped my backpack, crouched down, and started sweeping up dirt with my hands.

"Sorry!" I told him. "I didn't mean to surprise you."

Silent Santos knelt down next to me. "I was moving these to the library so they would get more sun."

If I was surprised to still be alive, I was even more surprised by his waterfall of words. I wanted to tease him and tell him to shut up already—but decided it probably wasn't a good idea.

Together, we scooped speckled potting soil and bright green seedlings back into their waxed paper cups while the other students slowly moved on. Some of them looked disappointed that they hadn't gotten to see me get stuffed into a trash can.

Remembering the way Silent Santos had jumped when I clapped my hands on Club Day, I wondered if he was always on edge because he had to fight so many people.

"Nice job on the math test," I said. "I usually get a perfect score, too. So which club did you end up joining?"

"None of them," he said.

"Well, which one did you think you were visiting when you came to my room?" I persisted.

"Gaming club."

"But you didn't end up joining that one, either?"

Silent Santos shrugged.

Finally, we had all the bean sprouts replanted. Hopefully, we had saved most of them.

"Debate Club still doesn't have any members, just in case you were wondering," I informed him as we stood up.

He nodded like it was no big surprise. As he turned and headed off to the library carrying his tray, I suddenly had an idea.

"Which is why it's not Debate Club anymore," I called after him. "I'm changing the name. From now on it's going to be called Detective Club. Because I have an amazingly impossible real-life mystery to solve!"

Silent Santos stopped halfway down the hall and slowly turned around. For the first time, he actually looked interested.

"What kind of mystery?" he asked.

chapter  22

AFTER I TOLD SILENT SANTOS HOW KERMIT AND Serenity had both been poisoned with an exotic toxin, and nobody had any idea why, he'd agreed to join Detective Club and meet me after school.

Now, as we walked to the Arcanum to continue the investigation, I explained what our jobs would be.

"I'll be the lead investigator, because I've done most of the sleuthing already," I told him, leaving out Detective Taylor for now. "I'm putting you in charge of security. If you haven't figured it out already, with a killer on the loose, this case could get dangerous."

Silent Santos didn't say anything, which wasn't

unusual, but the *way* he didn't say it caught my attention. I was getting better at reading his body language.

"Is there a problem with that?" I asked.

He nodded.

I was just about to ask what it was, but then I remembered something. When Detective Taylor asked questions, he let the silence build until the other person felt like they just *had* to say something. It was a good way to get answers.

Silent Santos wasn't most people, of course, because he was already used to letting others do the talking. But as I closed my mouth and gave him his own taste of the silent treatment, I could see him searching for words.

Finally, two blocks later, he cracked.

"I have anxiety," he said.

"What does that mean?" I asked.

"Well, lots of things make me nervous. Talking, mostly, but also meeting people and going new places. I hate loud noises. I'm even afraid of the dark."

"What happens when you feel anxious?"

"My heart beats really fast, I get dizzy, and I can't decide what to do. Usually, I just freeze, but sometimes I pass out."

We stopped at a red light across the street from my block. While we waited, I looked over at Santos. He was so big and tall that I had to take two steps back just to see all of him.

"It must be hard to make friends when everyone is afraid of you," I said.

"I could never hurt anybody," he said, sounding worried. "And if there's any scary stuff in this case, I think you'll have to handle it. Does that mean I can't be in Detective Club?"

I told him not to worry about it. But now I had another mystery to solve. If Santos was only going to be my silent partner, how could he help me?

As the DON'T WALK signal changed to WALK, I heard wheels clicking on the sidewalk. Heck pulled up on his scooter and crossed the street alongside us.

"What are you guys doing?" he asked, looking up at my new friend with wide eyes.

Santos actually smiled. "I'm in Minerva's Detective Club."

"You have a Detective Club? Why didn't you tell me?" asked my brother. "I want to be in it, too!"

"Okay, *fine*," I told him.

But as we walked into the Arcanum, I started having second thoughts. If one member of Detective Club was my accident-prone little brother, and the other one was a kid who was afraid of new people, new places, and even the dark, what chance did we possibly have against the killer on the loose in my building?

chapter 23

Bizzy was home, so I talked her into helping us practice our interviewing skills. I made her sit on a hard-backed chair in the middle of the living room while Heck, Santos, and I lined up on the couch across from her. I even tilted a reading lamp so it would shine in her eyes—I saw that one in the movies.

"State your name, please," I told her.

"Elizabetha Amaryllis Burnham."

"Can you *prove* that's your real name?" asked Heck suspiciously.

"Sure," said Bizzy, handing him her University of Chicago student ID.

While Heck squinted at it like he was trying to spot a forgery, I nodded at Santos, encouraging him to tackle the next question.

He took a deep breath. "Where were you on Saturday afternoon?"

Bizzy thought for a moment and then shook her head. "I have no idea."

"I'll give you a clue," I said. "You lost your shoes."

"Did you find them?" she asked hopefully.

"I was just trying to jog your memory," I told her. "Do you remember where you were when you lost your shoes?"

Bizzy looked a little bit sad. "Those were my favorite shoes. If I could remember where I was, I'd probably be able to find them."

"Never mind the shoes!" I said, exasperated. "Where did you spend most of that day?"

Bizzy frowned into the distance as she tried to bring back the memory.

"Remember how you told us you met with your dissertation advisor and decided on a title?" prompted Heck.

"Well, in that case, I guess I was at school," said Bizzy. "But it seems weird that I would have been there on a Saturday."

We weren't getting anywhere, so I decided to end the interview. I just hoped our neighbors were better at remembering where they were three days ago than my spacey cousin.

Heck, Santos, and I rode the elevator up to twelve, Kermit's floor. We needed to talk to his neighbors to find out what connected him to Serenity.

Heck wanted to do the knocking, and Santos wanted to stand as far away as possible, which left me in the middle. But even though Heck pounded on the first door like he was trying to break it down, nobody answered.

"Maybe they're still at work," he said.

"Let's keep going," I said.

The next door, 1202, was opened by a bald guy whose T-shirt was stretched so tightly across his muscles that if he flexed them, the shirt would probably snap and fly off like a rubber band.

"Don't bother trying to sell me cookies," he

said with a scowl. "Do you think I got this amazing body by eating *cookies*?"

He slammed the door in our faces before I could even ask him about Kermit and Serenity.

"Do we look like Girl Scouts?" Heck yelled.

Santos had already run halfway down the hall.

"Resident in 1202 seems aggressive," I wrote in my notebook. "Possible suspect?"

As we worked our way around the twelfth floor, things didn't go at all how I'd imagined: Half the people weren't home, and the other half wouldn't talk to us.

Serenity's floor wasn't much better. One old lady also thought we were selling cookies—and she wanted to buy some.

"Why, I would *love* some Girl Scout cookies!" she exclaimed. "Let me get my checkbook."

"We're not Girl Scouts," I called through the doorway as she disappeared inside her apartment. "We're detectives!"

She didn't hear me. Her hearing aids were squealing so loudly I could hardly hear myself.

"I hope you have Tagalongs, because those are my favorites," she said when she came back.

"WE DON'T HAVE COOKIES," I said as loudly as I could without yelling.

(Okay, maybe I was yelling a little.)

Her eyes were as big as cue balls behind her thick glasses as she held out a check. "I'll order one box of every kind you have. I left the amount blank, so you can just fill it in."

I tried to swat Heck's hand away but he was too quick. He snatched the check out of the old lady's hand.

"I'm going to go bake some cookies," said Heck after she closed the door. "This Detective Club could be a real moneymaker."

"I should probably go home, too," said Santos.

I couldn't believe they were both leaving. We still hadn't interviewed a single potential witness! Detective Club was on its way to becoming a complete and utter failure.

chapter  24

"**A**T LEAST TRY THE TENTH FLOOR WITH ME BEFORE YOU go home," I begged Santos. "*Someone* has to know something."

I could tell he didn't want to, but he reluctantly agreed, saying, "You do the talking. Your neighbors are strange."

We went down one floor while Heck continued on to our apartment, planning to bake cookies and cash in on the hungry old lady. I wondered what she'd think when her cookies showed up in paper bags instead of cardboard boxes.

No one was home in Apartment 1001, but when I knocked on 1002, a well-dressed man opened the door with a smile.

"I'm Minerva Keen and this is Santos Salgado," I told him. "Do you have time to answer a few questions? It's really important."

"My name is Young-Jae Park," he said. "Please come in."

I tried to record every detail with my eyes as we walked in, just like Detective Taylor. It wasn't easy: Mr. Park's apartment was cluttered with so many old things he could have opened his own antique mall.

On the mantel over the fireplace was a big brass sculpture of Lady Justice. She holds scales for weighing the arguments of both sides and carries a sword to show that she's boss and her decisions are final. She also wears a blindfold, meaning she'll treat you fairly no matter who you are.

"Do you like her?" Mr. Park asked when he saw me looking.

"A *lot*," I told him.

"Me, too," he said. "That's my favorite piece. Now, how can I help you?"

I took out my notebook and pen, ready to write down his answers.

"You probably heard what happened to your neighbors Kermit Hermanson and Serenity Meadows. We're trying to find out if there's a connection between them."

"Would you like something to drink?" Mr. Park asked suddenly. "I have homemade lemonade."

"Yes, please," I said.

After he left the room, Santos whispered, *"Don't drink it!"*

"Why not?"

"Maybe he's the poisoner. Don't you think it's suspicious that he let us in, then changed the subject as soon as you told him why we're here?"

Maybe Santos had a future as a detective, after all.

When Mr. Park came back with three glasses of lemonade on a tray, I realized that even though he was wearing nice clothes, nothing matched. His jacket was plaid, his tie was paisley, his shirt was a loud Hawaiian print, and his shorts had polka dots on them. Even his socks were different colors. It looked like he had gotten dressed in the dark.

As we all sat down around his coffee table, Santos and I put our glasses down without taking a sip. Mr. Park drank half his glass before continuing.

"Now, who are you, and what can I do for you?" he asked.

I raised my eyebrows at Santos. It was like our host had already forgotten everything I'd told him when we arrived.

"We're wondering if you knew Kermit Hermanson and Serenity Meadows," I reminded him.

"Well, I really didn't know Kermit," said Mr. Park. "But I was a member at Serenity's gym. What happened to her was such a tragedy."

"Did she ever talk about Kermit?"

"Not that I can recall."

"Do you remember if she had any enemies?"

Mr. Park loosened his tie with both hands, like it was strangling him. He seemed to be having trouble breathing. "If who had any enemies?"

"Serenity."

"No, but I *was* a member of her gym."

We were going around in circles. Either Young-Jae Park had even worse short-term memory than Bizzy, or there was something wrong with him. As I watched beads of sweat break out on his pale face, my heart started beating harder as I realized I already knew the answer.

Because Kermit had acted the same way just before he collapsed.

"Mr. Park, are you feeling okay?" asked Santos as our host took another big drink of lemonade.

"I'm fine," he said. "Remind me who you are again?"

I took out my phone. "I think we should call 911."

Mr. Park chuckled weakly. "Oh, there's no need for that," he said. "I'm just a little under...under..."

And with that, he fell face-first onto his coffee table, scattering the glasses and spilling lemonade everywhere!

chapter 25

"CALL 911!" I SAID. I PUT MY PHONE IN SANTOS'S HAND and wrapped his fingers around it.

Santos stared at Mr. Park with a look of horror. Our friendly host was sprawled across his coffee table like a badly dressed starfish.

I knelt down to check if Mr. Park was still breathing. The thick glass of the tabletop was fogged near his nose and mouth, so I guessed he was still alive.

My knees were soaking wet—the puddle of lemonade was still spreading.

Santos was holding my phone like it was a hand grenade.

"I can't call people I don't know," he said. "The only time I do it is when I'm ordering pizza."

But now Mr. Park was starting to slide off the table! I swept the sticky glasses out of the way so he wouldn't fall on them, then put my arms under his shoulders and helped him down to the floor.

"Then just...pretend...you're ordering...a pizza," I said. I was grunting like a weight lifter—Mr. Park was *heavy*.

Santos blinked, snapped out of his trance, and pressed the numbers.

I was rolling Mr. Park onto his back when I heard a woman's voice from the tiny speaker on my phone.

"What is your emergency?" she asked.

"I'd like a large thin-crust pepperoni, an order of cheesy garlic bread, and a side of ranch dressing," said Santos.

"Listen, kid, making a prank call to 911 is a felony offense," said the dispatcher angrily.

Santos stared at the phone like he couldn't believe what he'd just said, either.

"I didn't mean you should actually order a pizza!" I hissed at Santos. "Put it on speaker and I'll talk!"

I pulled a cushion off the couch and tried to remember my first-aid training from summer camp. Was I supposed to put it under Mr. Park's head or his feet?

"I'm hanging up now," said the dispatcher.

"Wait!" yelped Santos. "I can do this. We need...help."

"Not a pizza?" she asked sarcastically.

Guessing *feet*, I lifted Mr. Park's legs and wedged the couch cushion under his heels. Even his shoes were mismatched: One was for golf and the other was for bowling.

"Start over," I told Santos. "Take a deep breath and let it all out."

Santos sucked in so much air that if his lungs were balloons, they would have popped. Then, talking faster than someone listing the side effects in a pill commercial, he said: "Amandrankaglassof-lemonadeandthencollapsedontohiscoffeetablein-frontofus."

119

"I understand," said the dispatcher, obviously a pro at talking to panicking people.

"Wethinkitmightbepoison," added Santos, just before he ran out of breath.

"And what is the location of the possible poisoning?" asked the dispatcher.

"Thelivingroom," Santos wheezed.

"The Arcanum," I reminded him.

While Santos passed that along and listened to her next question, still using my phone, I held out my hand and whispered, "I need your phone."

He seemed totally confused. But he unlocked his phone and handed it to me anyway.

Taking Detective Taylor's business card out of my pocket, I dialed the number he had written on the back.

He answered: "Wesley Taylor."

"Minerva Keen," I said, trying to sound just as professional.

"How did you get this number?" he asked.

"You gave it to me last night," I reminded him. "Right before you told me to find something you don't already know."

"And did you?"

"I found the next victim: Young-Jae Park, in apartment 1002."

While I was talking, Santos bent over Mr. Park and touched his neck. He still had my phone to his ear, so I guessed the dispatcher was telling him how to check for a pulse.

Detective Taylor suddenly sounded a lot more interested. "And how did you do that?"

"I was questioning him when he collapsed right in front of me," I said. "I'm with him now. We already called 911. He's still alive...but we need help fast."

"I'm on my way," he said, hanging up.

My panicking partner Santos was once again as motionless as the body on the floor. He stared at me with big round eyes.

"What is it?" I asked.

"I think Mr. Park's heart just stopped."

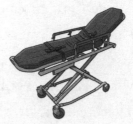

chapter 26

"His heart stopped?" I repeated.

I had heard Santos perfectly well the first time, but I needed time to think.

"I checked his pulse, just like the lady on the phone told me, and I couldn't feel anything," he said. "Now she says she's going to tell me how to do CPR!"

Santos tossed my phone to me but I threw it right back.

"So do it, then!" I told him.

He swatted my phone right back without even catching it. It was like he had pulled the pin out of a hand grenade and neither of us wanted to be holding it when it went off.

"I can't!" said Santos. "What if I do it wrong? What if I push too hard and break his rib cage, and one of the ribs stabs him in the heart, and he dies, and it's all my fault?"

"That will never happen!" I said, batting the phone to him.

The truth was that I was afraid to do CPR, too. When I'd gone to Camp Lost-in-the-Woods the previous August, we all had to take a first-aid course from the ancient Nurse Edith. To pass her test, every single camper had to demonstrate mouth-to-mouth resuscitation by breathing into the creepy rubber CPR practice dummy...and I was last in line. I was so grossed out that I threw up in its mouth. After that, the other kids all called me Barf Girl.

But when Santos returned my phone a third time, I realized I didn't have a choice. I got down next to Mr. Park again, set my phone on the coffee table, and put it on speaker.

"Tell me what to do," I said to the dispatcher.

"Place your hands in the middle of his chest, one on top of the other," she began. "Using your body's weight to help you, push down at least two inches. Quickly now: one, two, three, four..."

She counted out the beat, which made me think of a song my mom likes to play when she's packing for a trip: "Rumor Has It" by Adele.

As I leaned over Mr. Park and began pumping his sternum in a steady rhythm, the words went through my head.

Rumor has it...rumor has it...rumor has it...

Or maybe it wasn't just in my head. Santos was looking at me like I'd lost my mind.

"Are you...singing?" asked the dispatcher.

"That's the radio," I lied. "Don't you recognize Adele's voice?"

"The ambulance will be there any minute," she said. "If your arms get tired, you can take turns."

"Take over," I told Santos.

He hesitated, then knelt opposite me. When I lifted my hands, he put his hands where mine had been and started pumping. Even though he *was* doing it a little harder than me, I was sure he wasn't going to break Mr. Park's rib cage.

Pretty sure, anyway.

I needed to mentally prepare myself for what came next. I really, really wanted to save this man's life—but I was also really, really afraid he'd have bad breath.

And I really, *really* didn't want to barf in his mouth.

"Okay, I'm ready to do mouth-to-mouth," I told the dispatcher.

"We don't really start with that anymore," she said after a moment. "Just keep going with the chest compressions."

I silently swore at Nurse Edith, who probably hadn't updated her first-aid workbook since World War I.

Then a miracle happened. Mr. Park coughed. His whole body convulsed, like he was trying to bring up a hairball—and then his chest started rising and falling on its own.

"He's breathing!" Santos and I both said at the same time.

The front door flew open, and Big Joan and Little John rushed in.

"You again," said Big Joan, scratching her skull tattoo.

"Is Mr. Park going to be okay?" I asked.

Instead of answering, she checked on Mr. Park, then helped Little John strap him onto a gurney. Mr. Park was gasping and his fingers were moving like he was playing an invisible piano. He was turning a strange blue-green color.

"It's going to be touch and go," said Little John as they wheeled him out the door. "If you believe in prayer, now's the time."

chapter 27

When the door closed behind the EMTs, it was so quiet that I heard a single drop of lemonade splat onto the floor.

"You saved his life, Minerva," said Santos.

"*We* saved his life," I reminded him.

He shook his head and looked at the floor. "I was so scared I could hardly think."

"You did great," I said. "Except for the part where you kept throwing my phone at me."

"What do we do now?" asked Santos.

After what had just happened, I was so wound up I could hardly stand still, and I couldn't tell what was racing faster: my heart or my brain. What *should* we do now? Detective Taylor and his team would be there any minute—but for the moment, there was no one to tell us what to do.

"Let's search for clues," I told Santos.

We snooped through the rest of Mr. Park's apartment and discovered that the whole place was just as cluttered with antiques as his living room. The shelves were packed with leather-bound books, vintage vases, and strange sculptures, and the walls were decorated from floor to ceiling with paintings, photographs, and posters.

"*Hoarders*, here we come," I groaned.

"We'll never find a clue in here," complained Santos behind me. "He has so much stuff I don't know where to start!"

I walked into a hallway where both walls were covered with framed photos of Mr. Park and his friends. In every single picture, he was the best-dressed man in the group.

So why did he look like he had crashed and burned on *Project Runway* today?

Detective Taylor arrived a few minutes later, followed by his crime-scene crew and a scientist in a white lab coat.

"Who's this?" he asked, looking at Santos suspiciously.

Santos's mouth looked like it wouldn't open without the Jaws of Life, so I answered for him.

"This is Santos Salgado. He's assisting me in my investigation."

Detective Taylor frowned. "Can you trust him to keep our findings secret?"

"His nickname isn't 'Silent Santos' for nothing," I said.

"We'll see," said Detective Taylor, taking out his notebook. "What have you got, Minerva?"

"Mr. Park was a member of Serenity's gym, but he didn't really know her or Kermit," I said while the detective scribbled. "He offered us lemonade and collapsed shortly after he drank some. If you ask me, his symptoms seemed a lot like Kermit's."

"Did either of you drink the lemonade?" asked Detective Taylor.

We shook our heads.

"Santos told me not to, because he thought Mr. Park might be the poisoner," I said. Then it hit me. "Santos, you might have saved our lives!"

Santos turned bright red while Detective Taylor inspected the puddles on the coffee table and floor.

"Look for a pitcher in the kitchen," he told the man in the lab coat. "Otherwise, you'll have to test these. The rest of you know the drill."

As the crime-scene crew got to work, Detective Taylor did something I had never seen him do before: He smiled.

At me.

"Good work, partner," he said. "If you hadn't been knocking on doors, Mr. Park might be dead by now. You've given him a fighting chance."

Partner? I felt like I was going to collapse on the coffee table myself—but from pride. Maybe I was a real detective, after all.

chapter 28

HECK HAD THROWN HIMSELF INTO HIS GET-RICH-QUICK baking scheme, and our kitchen counters were covered with mixing bowls, wire racks, and freshly baked cookies. The latest batch was currently browning in the oven.

"I love the smell of sugar and money," said Heck, whose cheeks and nose were dusty with flour. "I hope the old lady likes coconut cranberry walnut crisps!"

"Are you cooking dinner tonight?" I asked.

He shook his head. "Not unless you've got a blank check lying around."

I picked up my phone and ordered from our favorite Chinese restaurant: sweet-and-sour pork, beef chow fun, vegetable fried rice, egg rolls, and egg-drop soup. I knew Heck would have ordered something with eggplant or pig intestines, but that was just too bad for him.

Bizzy arrived at the same time as the food. I introduced Santos and told her about Mr. Park while we all set the table and got ready to dig in to the delicious-smelling cartons. She seemed especially fascinated by his mismatched clothes and his antique-cluttered apartment.

"It's hard to imagine three more different people than Kermit, Serenity, and Young-Jae," said Bizzy as she put three chopsticks in front of my seat. "What's your latest theory on why they were poisoned?"

"I think an evil real estate developer is trying to kill all the residents one by one so he can buy their apartments and take over the building," said Heck.

Bizzy frowned and put a single chopstick in front of Santos's seat. "But why?"

"Money, obviously," said Heck. "This would make a killer four-star hotel. If they're working their way down from the top of the building, we have to stop them before they get to us."

I followed Bizzy around the table with plates, moving chopsticks to make sure we each had two of them. Eating with one chopstick is harder than dancing on one leg.

"Well, I'm starting to wonder if the Arcanum is actually a safe house for political refugees," I said.

"That might make sense for Kermit," said Bizzy. "And I think Young-Jae is Korean, so it's theoretically possible he's an enemy of the North Korean dictator. But who on Earth would have been targeting Serenity?"

"Junk food companies? People who hate exercise?" I guessed.

Our cousin wasn't finished. "And if this building really is a safe house, what are your parents hiding from?"

Heck was so excited that he dropped the napkins. "Maybe Mom and Dad are secret agents!"

I wanted to believe it, but that was just too farfetched. A mathematician and a philosopher as secret agents? *Please*. Although it *might* explain why they traveled all the time...

"Maybe a crazy person is just poisoning people for fun," said Santos quietly.

That shut everyone up. We all sat down and started scooping food onto our plates.

I was starving. I picked up a humongous piece of sweet-and-sour pork and was about to shovel it into my mouth.

Then Bizzy said, "Well, whoever it is, if they're poisoning food, and they're going after people who live in the building, then we could be next, right?"

I stared at the hunk of meat on my chopsticks, glistening with delicious orange sauce. Was it also dripping with...poison?

Everyone else was staring at their food, too.

One by one, we all put our chopsticks down—even Heck, which surprised me. With all the weird stuff he eats, I wouldn't have expected him to be afraid of a little poison.

Then I realized that something had been bothering me ever since we left Mr. Park's apartment. There *were* clues—and they had been staring us right in the face.

Number one, he was confused and forgetful even *before* he brought out the lemonade. Now that I thought about it, Kermit had been acting funny before he had his cake and tea, too.

Number two, the usually well-dressed Mr. Park was as mismatched as a thrift-store mannequin.

Which meant that he had been poisoned even before he got dressed.

So it couldn't have been in the lemonade.

I picked up the big piece of sweet-and-sour pork again, crammed it into my mouth, and started chewing. The taste was absolutely to die for.

Heck, Bizzy, and Santos stared at me like I'd suddenly grown tentacles.

"Trust me, it's fine," I said.

Heck didn't even ask why the food wasn't poisoned—he just picked up his chopsticks.

"If I'm gonna die, I'm not gonna die hungry!" he said gleefully.

Bizzy tried to taste her egg-drop soup, but since she accidentally used her fork, she didn't get very much in her mouth.

Santos took a tiny bite of his egg roll and chewed it slowly, looking like he expected to fall facedown in his food any minute.

After I explained my logic, though, even Bizzy and Santos started to relax and enjoy the meal. I was sure it was safe—well, ninety-nine percent sure. I still had one nagging question.

If people weren't being poisoned through their food, then *where was the poison coming from*?

CASE FILES

Name: Young-Jae Park

Occupation: Actuary.
(I don't know what that is.)

Relationship to case: Third poisoning victim

Hair: Black

Eyes: Brown

Age: 40 (approximately)

Identifying characteristics: Extremely well-dressed...
except when he isn't!

Personality: Outgoing, friendly, fun

Habits, behavior & special talents: Social butterfly.
Loves spending time with friends. Knows all the
best restaurants, theaters, and museums in
Chicago.

Lemonade

OOOOPS!

DETECTIVE'S NOTES:

Young-Jae Park might be the best-dressed man at the Arcanum. So when he greeted us wearing completely mismatched clothes, it should have been obvious something was wrong.

If only I had figured it out in time!

I thought the lemonade was the important clue when I should have been looking at his shoes.

(Well, I DID look at his shoes, but I still missed the clue.)

But if people aren't getting poisoned by their food, how is it happening?

More importantly, WHY IS IT HAPPENING???

chapter 29

AFTER DINNER, I WENT INTO MY ROOM AND CALLED the hospital to find out how Mr. Park was doing. Santos had gone home, Heck was baking cookies, and Bizzy was singing in the shower. Even though my door was closed, she was just as loud as if I was playing Spotify in my room—if Spotify played songs out of key and with random lyrics.

"Are you a relative of Mr. Park's?" asked the woman who answered the phone at the hospital.

"No, but I'm his neighbor," I said.

"We can only share information with family members," she told me.

"And what if he doesn't have any?"

"That still wouldn't make you related, now, would it?"

The woman on the phone obviously liked to argue just as much as I did. I would have to bring my A game.

"What if I told you that I saved Mr. Park's life today?" I asked.

"I wouldn't believe it," she said. "You're obviously just a kid."

Now she was making me mad.

"Voices can be misleading," I said. "What if *you're* just some stupid kid who happens to sound like an annoying adult?"

"Is there anything else I can help you with?" she asked in an ice-cold voice.

"WHO SAYS KIDS CAN'T SAVE LIVES?" I yelled.

She hung up on me. Yelling never helps win an argument.

When I called back, I disguised my voice. I pinched my nose with my left hand and wiggled my voice box with my right hand. I sounded like an old lady riding a paint mixer.

"Kermit Hermanson's room, please," I quavered.

"I'll put you through to the nurse's station, ma'am," said the operator politely. Since I had proved that you can't tell how old someone is just by hearing their voice, I declared myself the winner of the argument.

When Nurse Rosamie answered, I spoke normally. "This is Minerva Keen. Do you know anything about a new patient named Young-Jae Park?"

"I don't, but this is a big hospital," she said.

"Well, can you tell me if Kermit has woken up?" I asked. "Has he made any new chess moves?"

"Not that I know of. I guess I can look at the chessboard."

Nurse Rosamie put me on hold. The waiting music was peaceful and relaxing. If you ask me, they should pipe Bizzy's singing into the hospital— *that* would make people want to get better and go home as soon as possible.

"I'm in his room," said Nurse Rosamie a minute later. "What should I look for? I play checkers, not chess."

"Well, at the start of the game, each player's pieces are lined up in two rows on their side of the board," I explained. "Look for any pieces that have been moved into new places."

"Well, there are two short pieces in the middle, one white and one black," she said.

Those were the pawns, where Kermit had blocked my opening move.

"There's also a white horse thingy in front of the rest of the white pieces," she added.

That was the knight I had brought out on my second move the last time I was here. If that was all, then Kermit hadn't woken up again.

"Are there any others?" I asked hopefully.

"Yes. A tall black piece with a pointy head. It's two spaces in front of the horse."

Closing my eyes and picturing the board in my head, I saw that Kermit had moved his bishop diagonally, taking a position in the center of the board.

I was relieved that Kermit had woken up and moved again.

But I was also puzzled...because what he had played didn't seem like him at all. He was targeting a lowly pawn, which made zero sense.

What was he doing?

chapter 30

I HEARD A *BUMP* OUTSIDE MY DOOR. THEN A *THUMP*. Then a *crash*, followed by so much noise it sounded like a velociraptor was trapped in the hall.

Bizzy's out-of-tune singing continued from the bathroom. Whatever it was, she obviously hadn't heard it.

I stuck my head out and saw Heck staggering toward me. He was holding his throat with both hands and his eyes were bulging with terror. My skin prickled with icy fear as he croaked, "Help... me..."

"What's wrong?" I asked, even though I was sure I already knew.

The poisoner had targeted us!

Heck's voice was a ragged whisper. "It...was in...my cookies!"

He slid down the wall, flopped onto his back, and started flailing like an electrocuted swimmer trying to do the backstroke.

"BIZZY! HELP!" I yelled.

Apparently she had water in her ears, because she kept on singing.

I couldn't believe that my own brother had become the poisoner's next victim. How had I been wrong about the danger to our food? I was so terrified I could hardly think. But I had already saved one life that day—it was time to save another.

Crouching down next to Heck, I put my hands on his chest and started doing compressions, making them extra deep and hard. I heard Adele's song in my head again.

Rumor has it...rumor has it...rumor has it...

Heck was turning red in the face, so I pumped even harder until he started coughing and gasping. Finally, he pushed me off and squirmed away.

"Stop it, Minerva!" he said. "I'm okay! I was just messing with you!"

It took me a moment to realize that my brother hadn't actually been poisoned. He was just being a jerk, playing a stupid joke.

But now I wanted to kill him myself. I balled my fist, ready to punch him so hard that his head would literally spin.

"Butt for brains!" I yelled.

"I didn't think you'd actually *believe* it," he whined as he scooted backward out of my reach.

I stalked toward him. "Why wouldn't I believe it? People are getting poisoned for real all around us."

Heck scrambled to his feet and ran. Just then, Bizzy opened the bathroom door to see what was going on. Heck crashed into the door and dropped like a box of rocks.

Too mad to even see if he was okay, I went back into my room and slammed the door.

"Good luck finding someone to help when you really do get poisoned," I yelled. "Because I won't bother!"

Heck didn't apologize until I was lying in bed with the lights out.

"Sorry, Minerva," he mumbled through the air vent.

"I might accept your apology in the morning, you moron, but not tonight," I answered back.

"I thought you'd know I was faking, since you were the one who figured out the food wasn't poisoned," he said.

"That's not the point," I said. "Tonight Santos and Bizzy made me realize something else. I've been so obsessed with helping Detective Taylor solve the mystery that I haven't taken the danger seriously."

"Me, either," admitted Heck.

"Well, we both should," I told him. "Until we find out who's doing this, and how, no one in the building is safe...including us."

chapter 31

Before school on Thursday, Heck left early to deliver his cookies to the old lady on the eleventh floor. He had baked twelve different batches, from chocolate-chip to coconut-cranberry-walnut to one that had dried pineapple and chopped jalapeño peppers.

"I call that one the Keen Surprise!" he said.

I hoped the old lady's sense of taste was as bad as her hearing.

Once he was out the door, I FaceTimed Mom and Dad. I had an important question to ask and I didn't want Heck distracting everyone. The first thing I saw when the call connected was Dad's face, dripping with sweat. Then I saw Mom holding a racket. They were outside on a tennis court.

"We'll have to keep this brief, Minerva," said Dad. "Your mother and I are tied at one set apiece and we only have the court for another thirty minutes."

"Don't you guys ever work?" I asked.

"Intellectuals don't always work nine to five, Minerva," said Mom.

"Heck thinks you guys are secret agents," I told them. "After all, you're gone all the time, and nobody really understands what you do."

Dad and Mom looked at each other and then burst out laughing. They were laughing a little *too* hard, if you ask me.

"That's the most ridiculous thing I've ever heard," said Dad after he caught his breath.

"Where is Heck, anyway?" asked Mom.

"Delivering cookies. It's his new business, even though he only has one customer."

"Good for him!" said Dad. "I like his hustle."

"Well, I have a job, too," I informed them. "I'm helping Detective Taylor. There have been two more poisonings in the building since Kermit. One of our neighbors even died!"

"I hope you're getting paid," said Mom. "It's not *really* a job unless you're getting paid for your work."

"Tell Heck to send us some cookies," said Dad, looking like he was practically drooling.

I couldn't believe it. My mom was asking about money, and my dad was more concerned about cookies than the murders happening in our very own building!

"Don't you think Heck, Bizzy, and I should move out until the case is solved?" I asked. "I think we're in danger."

Dad sighed. "Let's look at this rationally. Out of the approximately two hundred people living in our building, three have been poisoned, one fatally—"

"That we know of," I interrupted.

"—meaning you have a point-oh-one-five percent chance of being poisoned yourself. And a point-oh-oh-five percent chance of being fatally poisoned. Those are *very* low odds."

It was always hard to argue when he started throwing numbers around.

"Has Detective What's-His-Name told you to move out?" asked Mom.

I shook my head. "Not yet."

"Then listen to your father," she said. "It's still extremely unlikely you'll be poisoned."

"Not in our building, it isn't!" I said.

"Just keep your wits about you and you'll be fine," said Dad, spinning his tennis racket impatiently. "We raised you to take care of yourself. Now if you'll excuse me, it's my turn to serve to your mother."

We ended the call. Maybe Heck was right and they were secret agents, after all. Who else would act like a one-in-two-hundred chance of getting fatally poisoned was no big deal?

chapter 32

A CARTOON WAS PLAYING ON THE WHITEBOARD AT the front of the classroom. I watched as a stick-figure lady uncapped a bottle of bleach and poured some of it into her mop bucket. Then she dumped in some ammonia. Stink lines rose out of the bucket, followed by a bunch of green frowny faces that I guess were supposed to be gas bubbles.

The cartoon lady looked surprised—then her eyes turned from Os to Xs and she keeled over.

"Danger under the sink!" said the video's narrator in a deep, dramatic voice. "Common household cleaners, such as bleach and ammonia, can create deadly toxic gas!"

"I think I smell some toxic gas now!" said the kid in front of me, making a farting sound.

Or maybe it was an actual fart. Either way, everyone laughed—except me.

I was bored out of my mind. Sure, chloramine gas was deadly, but it was easy to avoid. And only a bonehead was going to drink drain cleaner, weed killer, bug spray, or any of the other chemicals the narrator had warned us about. What I needed was information on the exotic poisons used in our building.

It's against the rules to use a phone in class, but whoever wrote the rules obviously wasn't thinking about murder cases. Keeping mine in my lap, I started Googling as fast as I could. Soon I had forgotten there was even a movie playing.

When the video ended, Mr. Boomershine turned the lights back on.

"ANY QUESTIONS?" he asked.

Mr. Boomershine is the health and PE teacher, and he also coaches the football, basketball, and soccer teams. His voice has only one volume level: REALLY LOUD.

I raised my hand. "Will there be a unit on exotic poisons?"

"WHAT DO YOU MEAN BY EXOTIC POISONS, MINERVA?" Mr. Boomershine boomed.

"You know, like botulinum, ricin, anthrax, and sarin," I said. "Everything from lab-created neurotoxins to naturally occurring poisons in animals. Did you know some frogs are so poisonous you can get paralyzed just by touching them?"

I had learned a lot in the last fifteen minutes.

Mr. Boomershine stared at me. Everyone else was staring at me, too.

"NO, WE WILL NOT BE DISCUSSING THOSE POISONS IN CLASS," he said. "DON'T DRINK BLEACH AND YOU SHOULD BE FINE."

"Shouldn't we be educated on *all* poisons, just to be safe?" I argued.

"WE DO NOT HAVE TO WORRY ABOUT POISON FROGS IN CHICAGO!" shouted Mr. Boomershine.

"But how do you know?" I asked.

"I'd be more worried about poison rats, if I were you," said the kid in front of me. "There are way more rats in Chicago than frogs."

"You can stop talking now," I told him as I shuddered.

It was bad enough knowing there were rats in Chicago without having to worry about poisonous ones.

After class, I texted Detective Taylor.

Have you identified the poisons used at our building yet?

We're still working on it, he wrote back. All we know so far is that each one was different.

Where does the poison even come from? I asked.

Solve that, and we solve the case, wrote Detective Taylor.

chapter 33

"HELLO? IS ANYBODY HOME? *HELLOOOOO?*"

I banged my fist on the elegant front doors of the Arcanum, but nobody answered. Cupping my hands around my eyes, I squinted through the glass and saw that Oskar wasn't at his desk.

Here's the thing about living in a building with a doorman: He opens the door for you, which is nice, especially when your hands are full. But if he needs to step away, he locks the doors to make sure nobody comes in and robs the place.

And even though we weren't robbers, now we couldn't get in, either. Heck and I never carry front-door keys—because we have a doorman.

I pulled on the big brass handles one last time, but the doors wouldn't budge. Then I turned around and shrugged at Heck and Santos.

"I guess he isn't there," I said.

"That's weird," said Heck. "I can't remember the last time Oskar was gone when I got home."

"Maybe he had to go to the bathroom," said Santos.

Santos had become a regular blabbermouth ever since joining Detective Club. Around other people, he was still about as talkative as a mailbox, but he acted differently with us. He had discovered that his vocal cords worked, and he liked using them, too.

"You're probably right," I told Santos.

While we waited for Oskar to finish his business, Santos and I watched Heck try to jump over a fire hydrant on his skateboard. Santos thought he would make it eventually, but I thought Heck would probably end up with a cast on his other arm, too.

Neither of us ended up being right. Ten minutes later, we were still stuck outside.

"I'll check the back door," Heck volunteered.

He pushed off and clickety-clacked down the sidewalk on his skateboard. As soon as he turned the corner, the front doors opened. But they weren't opened by Oskar, holding them wide and grinning at us like he always did.

Instead, a wild-eyed woman ran right into us, knocking us over like bowling pins. By the time I got back on my feet, she was halfway down the block.

"Stop!" I yelled.

She glanced over her shoulder and kept going. I don't think she could have run any faster if she was being chased by hungry cheetahs.

I pulled out my phone to take her picture, but she was already too far away.

Who was she?

chapter 34

Santos caught the doors before they slammed shut and locked again.

"Was that one of your neighbors?" he asked.

"I've never seen her before," I told him.

The way she had run out of the building definitely *seemed* suspicious, so I opened my notebook and wrote down everything I could remember about her. I hadn't gotten a good look at her face, but I knew she had curly hair and glasses. She was wearing a dark blue shirt, gray sweatpants, and white gym shoes.

Gym shoes are an excellent choice if you're planning to run away from the scene of a crime.

"We'd better find Oskar," I said.

He wasn't in the entryway, the lounge, or the atrium. Santos even looked in the men's bathroom. But there were no signs of life on the entire first floor.

Delores DeWitt's door was closed, but I doubted Oskar would have been in her office—he didn't like her any more than I did. ·

Then I remembered something. In addition to opening the front doors and signing for packages, it was also Oskar's duty to empty the lobby trash cans into the dumpsters in the basement. What if he was lying at the bottom of the stairs with a broken leg?

I led Santos to the basement door and opened it. The narrow wooden staircase was so dimly lit that we could hardly see the bottom.

"You first," I told Santos.

He shook his head. "I'm afraid of the dark, remember?"

"Well, I'm afraid of rats! Oskar told me he saw a rat down there."

"He's your doorman," said Santos. "I don't have a doorman, but if I did, I would definitely go looking for him."

I swallowed hard and put my foot on the first step. When a rat didn't bite my toes off, I kept going.

The Arcanum has marble floors, fancy fireplaces, and crystal chandeliers. But the basement seems like it belongs to a different building: the floor is hard-packed dirt, the furnace looks like it could come to life and eat you, and the only light comes from a couple of ancient light bulbs dangling from the ceiling.

If a Hollywood director wants to film a horror movie in Chicago, I've got the perfect place.

"Oskar? Are you down here?" I called.

My voice disappeared into the darkness. I didn't even hear an echo.

Then, above us, there was a RATTLE like something was falling a hundred miles an hour— and a deafening BANG when it landed. It sounded like a loaded dishwasher falling into the back of a dump truck.

Santos and I both screamed and tried to jump into each other's arms—meaning we crashed into each other and fell down.

"*What was that?*" whispered Santos.

"Just a bag of trash," I said as my terror slowly turned to relief.

It must have been dropped into the garbage chute by someone on a high floor. The bag had landed so hard, it was a miracle it hadn't exploded on impact, spraying us with wet coffee grounds and soggy banana peels.

"I won't tell anyone we screamed if you won't," I told Santos as we dusted ourselves off and stood up.

But I knew my secret was safe: He wasn't Silent Santos for nothing.

As we started walking toward the dumpsters, I listened hard, hoping I wouldn't hear another garbage bomb screaming down toward us. Then I burped, so deeply I could taste the cheese sandwich I had for lunch.

Santos stepped backward, waving the smell away with his hand.

"I can't help it," I said. "I burp when I'm nervous."

Then, from the darkness, we heard *someone else* burp.

"Oskar?" I called. "Is that you?"

It was completely silent—so silent that I burped again, even louder this time, and tasted the strawberry yogurt I ate for breakfast.

I turned on my cell phone's flashlight and started inching toward where I had heard the answering burp. Santos let me go first, using me as a human shield. The bright white light flashed on blue dumpsters...and a tiny shape on the floor in front of them.

When the tiny shape moved, my heart almost stopped.

"Is that a...*rat*?" I whispered.

Santos peered out from behind me. "I think it's a frog."

"What would a frog be doing down here?"

The frog hopped away and disappeared behind the dumpsters. We followed, trying to get a better look.

And then we saw it: a pair of shoes.

And not just any shoes. Oskar's shoes. With Oskar's feet in them. Oskar was lying as still as death.

I screamed and dropped my phone.

Santos fainted and fell over.

And when my phone hit the floor, the light went out.

chapter 35

I TRIED NOT TO PANIC AS I SEARCHED THE DIRT FLOOR for my phone. Even though there was a dim glow from a faraway light bulb, I couldn't see it anywhere. I must have accidentally tapped the flashlight button before I dropped it.

Finally, I found it—under Santos. I shook him but he didn't move.

I dialed 911 with quivering fingers, but I had zero bars and the call didn't go through. Leaving Santos and Oskar, I sprinted across the basement floor, raced up the rickety stairs—and ran smack into Delores DeWitt.

"What were you doing downstairs?" she demanded.

"I just found Oskar," I told her. "Something is wrong with him!"

Instead of asking *what* was wrong, she glared at me and said, "You just love trouble, don't you?"

Then she steered me to a chair and pushed me down so hard it was like she was trying to close a suitcase with too much stuff in it.

"Sit right there and *don't move*," she snarled as she dialed 911 from the front desk.

Even though I hated to leave Santos and Oskar in the basement, I felt too afraid to go back down there. What if a frog jumped out at me? Or a rat bit me?

What if a murderer *murdered* me?

But if my friends were in danger, I couldn't just sit in the lobby, having a stare down with Delores.

When she put the phone down, I stood up.

"I'm going to check on Santos and Oskar," I said.

Delores shoved me back into the chair. "You've gotten into enough trouble for one day!"

I kept standing up, and she kept pushing me down, until an ambulance screeched to a halt outside. The brother-and-sister EMT team hurried in.

"What is going *on* in this building?" asked Big Joan.

"I'd like to know that myself," said Delores, looking at me like she was judge, jury—and couldn't wait to play executioner.

When they came back upstairs, Santos was strapped onto the gurney. His eyes were still closed.

"He just passed out," said Little John. "He's going to be fine."

"That's my friend Santos—the real victim is behind the dumpsters," I told them.

Big Joan and Little John looked at each other like they were thinking, *Just how many bodies are in this building?*

"Well, we'd better wake this one up, because we only brought one gurney," said Big Joan.

She broke a capsule of smelling salts under Santos's nose and his eyes popped open like someone had poured ice water in his underwear.

Little John started questioning Santos. "What's your name, kid? Do you remember what day it is? Who's the president of the United States?"

Santos just looked at him and didn't answer.

Little John shook his head sadly. "He's lost the ability to speak."

"He's fine," I said. "He just doesn't like to talk to people he doesn't know."

"If you're finished messing around, you might want to go back downstairs," Delores said impatiently. "There's a dead man down there."

Santos climbed out of the gurney and sat down next to me, checking himself for bruises. "I don't think I like being a detective," he said.

As the EMTs went back down to the basement, I turned to Delores. "How do you know Oskar's dead? He could just be passed out, like Santos was."

She stabbed her finger at me like she wanted to poke my eye out. "Because everywhere you go, you leave bodies behind!"

Like they were proving her point, Big Joan and Little John came slowly up the stairs. They looked sad and serious. I saw Oskar's shoes sticking out from under the sheet—and the sheet was pulled over his head.

CASE FILES

Name: Oskar Błaszczykowski

Occupation: Doorman

Relationship to case: He saw everyone coming and going from the building. Did he know something he never got to tell us?

Hair: Blond, flat as a table on top

Eyes: Blue, very friendly

Age: Too young to get poisoned!

Identifying characteristics: Wore a suit jacket with "The Arcanum" stitched onto the pocket

Personality: Friendly and trustworthy

Habits, behavior & special talents: Knew what you needed before you did. If it was going to rain, he handed you an umbrella on your way out the door.

DETECTIVE'S NOTES:

It's not easy to be cheerful when your job is opening doors, signing for deliveries, and carrying groceries—but Oskar sure made it look easy.

He even made it look easy getting along with Delores DeWitt, something most people would find impossible. (I mean, how many people work for someone who's basically a witch?)

Some Arcanum residents treated him like part of the furniture, but not me. We were friends. He always remembered my birthday (March 15), so I made sure to remember his (September 29).

But he'll never have another birthday.

He always said, "If you want to see the rainbow, you gotta put up with the rain."

Do you know who said that originally? Dolly Parton!

Oskar was a secret country music fan!

chapter 36

I STOOD ON THE SIDEWALK IN FRONT OF OUR BUILDING with Santos, watching as the EMTs loaded Oskar into the ambulance. For once, Big Joan didn't burn rubber when she drove away—she just eased out into traffic without even bothering to turn on the siren and flashing lights. Poor Oskar was dead.

"Well, I guess you're happy now," said Delores behind me.

"He was my friend!" I said, wiping tears off my cheeks. "What is *wrong* with you?"

She shrugged. "Nothing—as long as you don't poison me, too."

Detective Taylor pulled up to the curb and double-parked. He was driving a black, unmarked car but he probably didn't have to worry about a ticket.

"How did Detective Taylor get here so fast?" I asked.

"I called him," said Delores smugly. "He gave me his card."

That hurt. Why would he give her his phone number, too? I was his partner—not Delores.

Detective Taylor crossed the sidewalk toward us.

"I hope you're ready to arrest this girl," announced Delores. "I don't know how she's doing it, but every time she shows up, somebody drops dead."

"Don't listen to her—she's crazy!" I told him. "We saw somebody run out of the building right before we found Oskar!"

Detective Taylor held out his hands like he was directing traffic. "Hold on and let me do my job, both of you. Ms. DeWitt, will you please return to your office until I've finished interviewing Minerva and Santos?"

"I will not," she said defiantly. "I'm going to stay right here to make sure she tells you the truth."

"Then I guess you don't mind letting Minerva sit in when I question you," said Detective Taylor.

Apparently Delores did mind, because she finally left. Santos looked like he wished he had his own office to go to.

Detective Taylor took us inside and asked us to sit down in the lounge. I noticed he was wearing a tie I had seen before—the ketchup-and-mustard one.

"I'm truly sorry to hear about Oskar," he said. "Are you both okay?"

"Of course not," I said, wondering if detectives like him ever got used to seeing so many horrible things. "You don't really believe Delores, do you?"

"Put her out of your mind for now. Just start from the beginning and tell me what happened," said Detective Taylor.

I took a deep breath and got ready to tell him everything we'd seen since we came home from school. But before I could even say one word, I started crying. And I'm not talking about a couple of teardrops or a few sniffles, either: I bawled like a baby until I was hiccupping snot out of my nose.

It was embarrassing, but I just couldn't stop. First Kermit, then Serenity, then Mr. Park, and now Oskar—Oskar, who had been the building's doorman since I was a little kid. He just didn't deserve to be poisoned. None of them did. Why was it happening? When would it all end?

"Take your time, Minerva," said Detective Taylor, offering me a box of Kleenex he found on Oskar's desk.

When I realized it was Oskar's personal box of Kleenex, I only cried harder.

Even Santos was crying a little—silently, of course.

By the time I was done, I had used half the box of tissues and Detective Taylor's crime-scene crew had arrived. One of them, a short guy with a pointy beard, was a sketch artist. I described the woman we had seen run out of the building, and Santos nodded in agreement or shook his head when he thought I was wrong. Soon the sketch artist had finished a drawing that looked just like her.

"Do you think that's the killer?" I asked Detective Taylor.

"Let's not jump to conclusions," he warned me. "We have to find her first."

Just then I heard the clickety-clack of Heck's skateboard, moving toward us from the back of the building. Heck zoomed out of the atrium with a red-faced cop running after him in hot pursuit. She caught up just as he tail-scraped to a stop.

"I found this kid trying to break in through the back door," said the cop, breathing hard.

"It's okay, he lives here," Detective Taylor told her.

"What did I miss?" asked Heck, as the cop threw up her hands in frustration.

I didn't know where to start.

"Minerva, would you leave me with Heck and Santos, please?" asked Detective Taylor. "I'd like to question you all individually before I speak with Delores."

I couldn't believe what I was hearing. My own partner was shutting me out.

chapter 37

I WAS SO ANGRY THAT I STOMPED OUT OF THE ARCAnum. After everything I had done to prove myself, why was Detective Taylor pushing me away? Had he changed his mind and decided I might be guilty after all?

Before I knew it, I was halfway to DuSable Hospital. I decided to check on Kermit again to see if he was getting better. I didn't know what I would do if I found out he was getting worse.

I hurried up to his room. His eyes were still closed, but his breathing was regular, and the doctors didn't seem to have plugged any more tubes and wires into him.

A glance at the chessboard told me he had woken up and moved again.

And now I saw what he was trying to do.

The last time, I had moved my other knight to protect my king. In response, he had brought out his queen, targeting the same pawn as his bishop. He was trying to force me into a Scholar's Mate and end the game!

But he must have been delirious, because he should have known I would never fall for something that simple.

Leaving his room, I found Nurse Rosamie at her station.

"Kermit keeps moving his chess pieces," I told her.

She smiled. "Well, that's a good sign, right? It means he's waking up."

"It *would* be a good sign if he was playing well, but he's playing like he has no idea what he's doing. What if he never gets better?"

"He's been through a lot, Minerva, and he's very old and sick. Be patient."

"Are you sure no one else is moving for him?" I asked.

Nurse Rosamie nodded her head firmly. "One hundred percent sure. I've asked, and none of the other nurses play chess, either."

I went back to Kermit's room. I had tears in my eyes as I moved my queen out to attack.

"*Please* wake up and get better," I begged.

But the old man slumbered on.

chapter 38

THE STREETLIGHTS WINKED ON AS I STARTED WALKING home. Dark clouds crowded the evening sky. Far away, I heard a rumble that was longer and louder than an L train—thunder.

My phone rang: Detective Taylor was calling.

"Why did you talk to Santos and Heck without me?" I asked when I answered. "Don't you trust me anymore?"

Detective Taylor chuckled. "Of course I still trust you. I just wanted to get their stories in their own words, without you doing the talking for them. I'm driving Santos home now."

Well, *that* was a relief.

"What did Delores tell you?" I asked.

"She ID'd the sketch," he said. "The woman is a housekeeper who last came to the building two weeks ago, so she couldn't have done the poisonings. She was running because she was late for her bus."

Big raindrops started splatting on the sidewalk. I was about to get soaked.

"There must be lots of cleaning ladies and dog walkers who visit the building every day—what about them?" I asked.

"I already thought of that," said Detective Taylor. "I had my team go over the visitors' log, but none of the cleaners or dog walkers were at the building for every incident, and none of them had keys to any of the victims' apartments."

Then, as the rain really started to pour, headlights flashed and a car pulled over next to me. Santos was waving at me from the front seat and Detective Taylor was behind the wheel.

"Get in. I'll give you a ride home, too," he said, lowering the window.

I climbed into the back seat and rode along as he dropped off Santos, who only grunted when I said, "See you at school tomorrow!" Then I rode in the front seat on the way back to the Arcanum.

"It's driving me crazy how Delores keeps trying to blame me for everything," I complained.

"Well, you have to admit, you do keep turning up at the scene of the crime," said Detective Taylor.

I slapped the dashboard. "Maybe it's her! Think about it: She's been in the building every single time, she has keys to every door, and she's definitely mean enough to poison people. If *you* were the killer, wouldn't *you* try to make someone else look guilty?"

"I suppose," he said thoughtfully.

"Also, she seemed to know Oskar was dead already—but I didn't know that until the EMTs brought him upstairs."

Detective Taylor pulled in front of the Arcanum and left the engine running. His windshield wipers could hardly keep up with the rain.

"Even if all that is true, people don't usually poison multiple victims for no reason at all," he said. "And I'll get laughed off the police force if I arrest someone just for being mean. What's her *motive*, Minerva?"

I didn't have an answer for that.

chapter  39

"BACK FROM THE POLICE STATION?" SNEERED DELORES.
"I guess he decided not to arrest you...yet."

Delores, of all people, was holding the door
open for me. She had seen me get out of Detective
Taylor's car.

"He just gave me a ride—in the front seat," I
told her. "When it's your turn, you'll be riding in
the back, wearing handcuffs."

"He'll find out your secret soon enough," said
Delores.

"I don't have any secrets," I said as I walked
past her. "In fact, maybe we should call a reporter
to tell them what's happening. Maybe if the TV
news did a big story about the poisonings at the

Arcanum, it would help us solve the case."

Delores turned pale. She closed the door so fast that I had to jump out of the way so it didn't hit me in the butt.

"Does that make you nervous?" I asked.

"Don't you dare call a reporter," she said, shaking her finger at me. "Bad publicity is bad for the building."

"Bad for *you*, you mean," I said over my shoulder. "By the way, your doorman skills need work."

"I'm just filling in for Oskar until a temp arrives!" she yelled.

In the atrium, I saw people setting up rows of chairs, like they were getting ready for a meeting.

A sign by the elevator explained:

CANDLELIGHT VIGIL TONIGHT

PLEASE JOIN US AT 8 P.M. THIS EVENING FOR A CANDLELIGHT
VIGIL TO HONOR YOUR ARCANUM NEIGHBORS WHO HAVE
RECENTLY PASSED AWAY OR FALLEN ILL.

FREDERICK FRIZZELL
PRESIDENT, ARCANUM CO-OP BOARD

I was glad to know someone in charge cared about Kermit, Serenity, Young-Jae, and Oskar— because Delores obviously didn't.

chapter  40

MY FIRST THOUGHT WHEN I WALKED THROUGH THE door of our apartment was that we had been robbed. All the cabinet doors were hanging open and all the drawers had been pulled out. Some of them were even lying on the floor.

My second thought was that we had been hit by a tornado. Because the stuff that had been in the cabinets and drawers was scattered all over the floor.

I ruled out the tornado first. I hadn't heard a tornado siren, and besides, it seemed unlikely that one would have come through our apartment without damaging the rest of the building.

The real culprit was in our living room.

Heck looked like a maniac on an Easter egg hunt. While I watched, he searched inside the TV cabinet, under the couch, and even behind the books in the bookcase.

"We can't go to the candlelight vigil without any candles," he said. "Do you know where we have any?"

"No," I told him. "Did you ask Bizzy?"

"She's helping me look."

I found Bizzy in the kitchen, where she was taking cans out of the pantry one at a time and stacking them on the counter.

"Did you find any?" I asked.

"Any what?" she said.

"Candles."

Bizzy stared at the can of tomato soup in her hand and then burst out laughing. "I had completely forgotten what Heck asked me to look for. But did you know that some of this food is past its expiration date?"

Some of our neighbors are past their expiration dates, too, I thought.

In the other room, Heck yelled, "BOOYAH!" and a moment later, he came sliding into the kitchen in his socks. Pushing Bizzy's cans out of the way, he dumped an armload of stuff onto the kitchen counter.

"I couldn't find a candle, but I have an idea that might be even better," he said. "I found this bottle in the recycling bin. We can fill it with the lighter fluid I found in the hardware closet. Then all we have to do is stuff this old rag into the bottle to make a wick. Light it, and voilà! Instant oil lamp."

I stared at him in horror. I expected Bizzy to shut him down, but she only nodded. "In my freshman anthropology class, I learned that people have made simple lamps like this for thousands of years."

I couldn't take it anymore.

"Are you both bonkers?" I asked. "That's not a lamp—that's a Molotov cocktail! If we take that downstairs, we'll set the whole building on fire."

While Bizzy and Heck Googled *Molotov cocktail*, I took one last look around the apartment for a candle. In the dusty fireplace of Dad's study, I found a massive pillar candle with four wicks—one for each of the poisoning victims.

I wrapped my arms around it, hoisted it, and carried it back to the kitchen. Heck and Bizzy were now reading the whole Wikipedia article about Molotov cocktails.

"I guess you're right, Minerva," said Heck. "A Molotov cocktail is the wrong thing to bring to a candlelight vigil. It's more of a weapon."

"I can't believe you had to read that whole thing just to know I'm right," I told him. "Fortunately, I found a candle we can use."

"Remind me what the candle is for?" asked Bizzy.

chapter 41

IT SEEMED LIKE THE WHOLE BUILDING HAD SHOWN UP TO the vigil in the atrium. Every chair was filled, so I stood in the back, sweating under the weight of my candle that was as big as a campfire log. People were giving me the stink eye, because now that all four wicks were lit, it smelled like a watermelon Jolly Rancher.

Everyone else was holding little white candles that had been handed out by a volunteer. Heck and Bizzy had each gotten one and were now acting like they didn't know me.

How were we supposed to know that candles would be provided?

Delores DeWitt was sitting near the front. Because I was standing up, I could see that the glow lighting her face didn't come from a flame—it came from the screen of her phone. I could *also* see that she was looking at Etsy.

She was so bored, she was shopping!

At eight o'clock, she put her phone away and stood up in front of a table displaying framed photos of Kermit, Serenity, Young-Jae, and Oskar.

"Many of you have complained to me about the recent poisonings," she told the crowd. "And I get it: You're afraid for your lives—and your property values."

Delores had been Oskar's supervisor for years, but she didn't sound sad at all. She sounded like a principal lecturing students about bad behavior. Then she spotted me and her voice got super dramatic.

"Remember that the murderer could be someone you'd never expect, even someone as innocent seeming as a schoolgirl," she said, locking her eyes on mine. "So until we catch her, stay alert. Report anyone you see snooping around or doing anything unusual. And *always* lock your doors!"

I squirmed as people started looking at me again. Delores had all but said I was guilty!

Then Fred Frizzell, the board president, stood up. His sad eyes and whiskered face reminded me of a seal in the Lincoln Park Zoo.

"Please join me in a moment of silence for our neighbors," said Fred solemnly.

As everyone else bowed their heads, I stared at the pictures on the table, thinking how strange it was to see all of them smiling and looking happy. I might have been the only one in the atrium who kept her eyes open...which was a good thing, since I saw that Delores was sneaking away!

I elbowed Heck, who opened his eyes.

We have to follow her, I mouthed.

He didn't need to be told twice. Leaving Bizzy, whose eyes were still tightly shut, we tiptoed through the crowd after Delores.

She *could* have been leaving because she was bored...or what if Delores was the murderer? With everyone in the atrium, it would have been easy for her to plant the poison for her next victim.

Unless we stopped her.

We watched as Delores hurried into the rear hallway. Before we followed her in, we blew out our candles. We couldn't let her see the flickering flames or have the smell of watermelon-flavored candy give us away.

Peering around the corner, we saw Delores skulk past her own office with exaggerated footsteps, like she was trying to be as quiet as possible. Our necks were stuck pretty far out when she suddenly stopped and whirled around.

Heck and I pulled our heads back as fast as we could.

"Do you think she saw us?" whispered Heck.

"If she did, we'll know in a minute," I whispered back.

But Delores didn't come back to find us.

When we looked again, she was at the far end of the hallway, pulling on the massive doors to our freight elevator. They seemed to be stuck. Then, all of a sudden, she almost fell over when they flew open.

She stepped inside and was gone.

chapter 42

"DELORES IS SMART," I TOLD HECK AS WE HURRIED down to the end of the hallway. "Evil, but smart."

The numbers on the elevator indicator were rising as Delores went up: 2...3...4...

"What do you mean?" asked Heck.

"She knows this is the perfect time to commit a crime, because nobody is watching—"

"Except us," said Heck.

...5...6...7...

"—and she reminded everyone to lock their doors, when *she's* the only one who has a key to every unit in the building!"

"Scary smart," agreed Heck. "But where is she going?"

We watched as the freight elevator continued to climb floors: *8...9...*

It finally stopped on 10. She was going after someone else on Mr. Park's floor!

I pushed the button and the elevator started coming back down. The building was so quiet that we could hear Fred Frizzell's voice echoing from the atrium. The moment of silence had ended.

"As we grieve for our neighbor Serenity, and our employee Oskar, and pray for the recoveries of Kermit and Young-Jae, all of them much-loved members of our community, it is important that we remember them as healthy, vibrant, and alive."

"We'll never catch up with her," complained Heck. "This elevator is so slow!"

When it came, we scrambled inside. Its doors opened from the top and bottom, not the sides, and its wooden floor was big enough to move a grand piano. We paced nervously as we rode up to the tenth floor.

On the balcony, every door was closed and Delores was nowhere to be seen.

"She has to be in one of those apartments," I said. "Maybe she forgot to lock the door behind her. You take that side and I'll take this side."

While Heck took off in the other direction, I turned the handle of the nearest door. It was locked and didn't budge.

Far below us, Fred Frizzell's kind words were interrupted by an angry shout.

"It's too bad about Oskar and the others, but what about the rest of us? Who will be the next to die?"

I looked over the railing and saw the big, bald bodybuilder shaking his fist at Fred. He lived on this floor...Delores could be in his apartment at that very moment!

Fred pleaded with him, probably hoping he wouldn't hulk out. "This is a candlelight vigil, not a co-op meeting."

As I continued turning doorknobs, I could hear arguments echoing up from below.

"We can't wait for the meeting," said the bodybuilder. "My picture could be on that table tomorrow!"

"We elected you our leader, Fred, so lead us," scolded a woman who sounded like the sweet old lady who'd bought Heck's cookies.

"Please calm yourselves!" begged Fred, as though the crowd was carrying torches and pitchforks, not little candles. "The detective in charge assures me he has his very best people on the case."

Was I one of Detective Taylor's "very best people"? I turned doorknobs frantically, racing from apartment to apartment, but so far, every single one was locked.

Where was Delores DeWitt?

Far below us, I heard chairs scraping as people began to storm out. The vigil was over.

Heck and I were about to meet up at the passenger elevator. We still had seen no sign of Delores. There was only one more door on my side to check: 1002.

Mr. Park's apartment.

I almost skipped it because he was already in the hospital, clinging to life. But a good detective leaves no handle unturned. Heck caught up with me just as I got there.

But before I could even touch the doorknob, it turned on its own. The door flew open and Delores DeWitt stepped out. She stared down at us with a wicked grin.

"Caught you!" she said.

CASE FILES

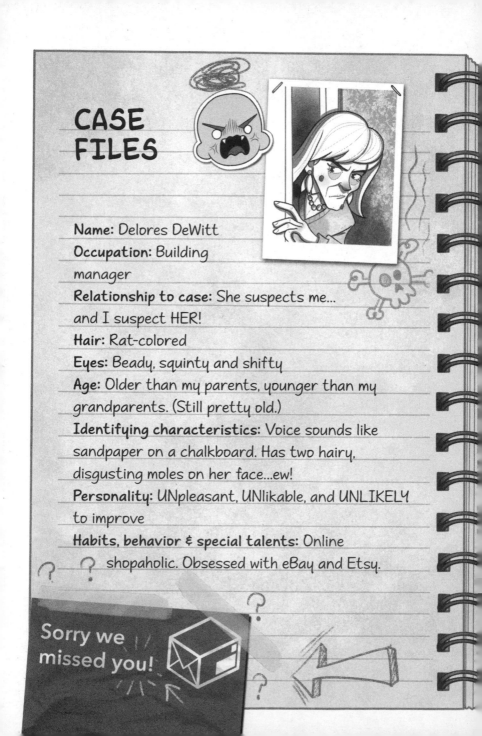

Name: Delores DeWitt

Occupation: Building manager

Relationship to case: She suspects me... and I suspect HER!

Hair: Rat-colored

Eyes: Beady, squinty and shifty

Age: Older than my parents, younger than my grandparents. (Still pretty old.)

Identifying characteristics: Voice sounds like sandpaper on a chalkboard. Has two hairy, disgusting moles on her face...ew!

Personality: UNpleasant, UNlikable, and UNLIKELY to improve

Habits, behavior & special talents: Online shopaholic. Obsessed with eBay and Etsy.

Sorry we missed you!

DETECTIVE'S NOTES:

Delores DeWitt is supposed to make sure everything runs smoothly at our building, keeping it clean and safe and well repaired.

But she actually spends all her time scaring babies, kicking dogs, and brewing poison. (I don't have proof of these things...but I WILL find it.) She definitely does not like kids. Or fun. Or kids who have fun.

I didn't know Delores as a kid—because I am not fifty years old—but if I did, we would not have been friends. Because I can tell that even when she was a kid she didn't like kids. She probably sucked up to grown-ups and tattled on other kids when they did something wrong.

I know Delores is guilty.

BUT HOW CAN I PROVE IT???

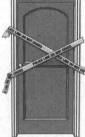

chapter 43

"ARE YOU KIDDING? *WE* CAUGHT *YOU!*" I TOLD DELORES.

"Doing what?" she asked innocently. "Checking to make sure the gas and water were turned off in an unoccupied apartment? That's my *job*."

"You were covering your tracks," I insisted, even though I knew Detective Taylor's crime-scene team had already combed the apartment for evidence.

"And *you* were breaking in," said Delores. "Which you can explain to your ditzy cousin—and to the police."

She locked Mr. Park's door with a key from a ring that was as large as a Nerf basketball hoop. Then she marched us to the passenger elevator. A handful of people spilled out as we arrived, but they were arguing and hardly seemed to notice us.

On the second floor, Delores rapped sharply on our door and waited for Bizzy to answer.

"Is everything okay?" asked our cousin when she saw us. "I opened my eyes and you were gone."

"That's because the little delinquents were breaking into Young-Jae Park's apartment!" said Delores triumphantly.

Bizzy's eyes widened. "Is this true?"

"Well, technically—" began Heck.

"NO!" I yelled.

"I'll be filing an official report, since I'm a witness," said Delores. "You seem to be a terrible guardian, but I hope you can at least keep them out of trouble until the police arrive to question them."

Bizzy appeared even more confused than usual. She looked at Heck, then at me, then at Delores, obviously unsure what to say.

"She will," I answered for her. "Won't you, Bizzy?"

"I guess so," said my cousin softly.

When Delores turned and walked away, I may or may not have made a rude face that definitely would have gotten me detention at school.

Bizzy followed us inside and closed the door. "What just happened?"

"Delores laid a trap for us," I said, mad at myself for walking right into it. "Either she saw us behind her or smelled my stupid candle. Then she waited until we caught up."

"Maybe after she got out of the freight elevator, she noticed it going down and realized we were coming up after her," suggested Heck.

I snapped my fingers. "Then she hid in Mr. Park's apartment so we wouldn't know who she's actually targeting next."

Bizzy sat down on the bench by our front door, took off one shoe, and stared at it. "I still don't understand."

"I think Delores DeWitt is the murderer," I told her.

"Do you have any evidence to prove that?" asked Bizzy.

"That's what we were trying to get," said Heck.

"But now you look guilty, too," said Bizzy, putting her shoe back on and tying it, like she forgot she'd just taken it off. "You shouldn't break the rules to catch someone else breaking the rules."

"Not even when it's life and death?" I asked.

"That sounds like a question for a philosopher, like your mom," she said. "I should probably ask your parents how they want me to handle this."

"Or you could wait a little while, until everything calms down," I suggested.

Heck gave me a worried look. Our parents don't like getting bad news when they're traveling.

Bizzy shook her head. "I'm going to give them a call. When they asked me to look after you guys, I never dreamed you'd actually get in trouble!"

chapter 44

"GROUNDED? WHAT DO YOU MEAN WE'RE GROUNDED?" I asked.

Heck and I were standing in the doorways of our rooms, staring at the phone in Bizzy's hands. Dad's furious face frowned out at us from its tiny screen. After Bizzy told him about the trouble with Delores, he didn't waste any time in punishing us.

I couldn't believe it. We had never *been* grounded before. It seemed like something that only happened to kids in books and movies.

"So how does it work?" asked Heck. "We just... stay home?"

"I don't want you to set foot out of the apartment for the next twenty-four hours," said Dad.

"Except for school, obviously," I said.

He shook his head. I wasn't sure I'd ever *seen* him so mad. "You're both going to stay home tomorrow and study with Bizzy. I've already received an email from Delores stating that you were trespassing in another resident's apartment and that she's reporting it to the police. This is serious, Minerva."

"This is total garbage!" said Heck.

Mom's face appeared as she took the phone from Dad. "Kids, this detective stuff is getting out of hand. I mean, do you *really* think the building manager is a murderer?"

"When she gets away with another one, don't blame us!" I yelled.

"Don't leave the apartment until we figure out what to do next," said Dad, taking the phone back. "And remember: while we're gone, your cousin is in charge. What she says goes."

The screen went black as he ended the call. Bizzy stood in the hallway looking miserable.

"I'm sorry, you guys," she said. "I don't like this any better than you do. But you'd better do what your parents told you."

Heck slowly closed the door to his room.

I slammed mine.

Bizzy has always been more like a big sister than a babysitter. Most of the time, I feel like I'm taking care of *her*. But now she was our warden—and we were her prisoners.

I grabbed my phone and texted Mom and Dad, spamming them with angry emojis. Everybody was treating us like we were just some stupid kids, when we were the only ones who really knew what was happening!

Through the vent, I heard computer keys clicking. Heck was online. I flopped down on my bed so I could talk to him.

"We're supposed to spend all day tomorrow with Bizzy?" I groaned. "While we're stuck inside, Delores can run around poisoning all the people she wants."

Heck's voice sounded distracted. "Don't worry about it."

"What do you mean, don't worry about it?"

"Tell Santos to pretend he's sick or something and meet us here tomorrow morning," he said. "I have a plan. Now excuse me while I make us a midnight snack."

"I don't want a snack," I told him, but he had already left his room. I could hear his footsteps going down the hallway.

How could he even think of eating at a time like this?

chapter 45

WHEN I WOKE UP ON FRIDAY MORNING, MY STOMACH felt as round and hard as a watermelon—it felt like I had *swallowed* a watermelon. I could hardly move without groaning in agony. Was this what it was like to be poisoned?

Heck opened the door to my room. His hair stuck out in all directions like someone had rubbed his head with a balloon.

"How are you feeling?" he asked.

"Like I'm about to explode," I told him.

"Good," he said.

Heck's "midnight snack" had been more like a death-row prisoner's last meal—if food was the method of execution. The three-course meal was the worst thing he had ever prepared in his life.

Huge pieces of raw broccoli and cauliflower.

Piles of three-bean salad made from under-cooked navy beans, pinto beans, and lima beans.

Bucket-sized cabbage-kale-arugula smoothies.

"Are you ready?" asked Heck.

"I just hope we don't kill ourselves," I said. "Or anyone else."

I climbed out of bed, feeling like the watermelon might shoot out of my butt at any moment. As we went down the hall, my stomach made a weird, echoey sound, like a demon yodeling in a cavern under a volcano.

Heck looked over his shoulder at me and grinned.

Bizzy was already awake and studying in the dining room. Her laptop, books, and papers covered the whole table.

"I'm going to have to ask you guys to be super quiet today, because I have an important deadline for my dissertation tomorrow," she said. "I really, really need to concentrate."

"We understand," I assured her.

Heck and I waddled over to the table like we were holding potato chips between our butt cheeks and trying not to break them. The pressure bloating my belly was painfully intense.

The night before, Heck had been researching which foods caused the most gas, and obviously, he had done his homework. We were poised to unleash the biggest fart-storm ever smelled in Chicago.

As the air turned foul with the aroma of rotten eggs and fancy cheese, I realized Heck had already let one slip—silent but deadly.

Bizzy wrinkled her nose and gagged. "Oh, god. Who did that?"

"Sorry," said Heck. "My stomach is upset. Probably because *I'm* so upset about missing school."

I fired next, a long, low, ripper that lasted a full thirty seconds and sounded like someone playing a trumpet with an air hose.

Parparaparparapa! Parparaparparapa!

I didn't even know it was possible to become nauseated by smelling your own fart, but it was true: The odor of swamp gas and hot roadkill made me want to barf, which made me fart again. This one came out rapid-fire, like bursts from a machine gun, each one stinkier than the last.

BLATBLATBLATBLATBLATBLATBLAT!

Now Heck was really letting loose. He rose out of his chair, propelled by his own gas, as he fired a salvo of disgustingly wet stink bombs.

Blert. BLAT. *BlipBLIPblipBLIPblipBLIP.* FWOSH!

"OH MY GOD, YOU GUYS!" shrieked Bizzy, pushing back from the table so hard her chair fell over. She ran to the nearest window, threw it open, and stuck her head outside. Her shoulders heaved as she sucked in fresh air.

We followed her, showing no mercy. I couldn't believe I had anything left in my stomach, but Heck, the gaseous gourmet, had outdone himself and it seemed like our farts would never stop. We weren't just breaking wind—we were destroying it.

"So sorry!" I told Bizzy. "I guess we're both feeling under the weather."

"Probably something we ate," said Heck, trying not to laugh.

"Get away from me!" she hollered, running into her room and slamming the door.

We waited outside, our nostrils burning and eyes watering from the clouds of toxic gas.

Flerb. Blort! BLAT. Porp. FLEBLEBLEBLEB!

Bizzy came out again, looking panicked, and shrieked, "I CAN SMELL IT EVERYWHERE!"

Coughing and gagging, she stumbled back to the table and started stuffing books and papers into her backpack.

"I can't stay here!" she said as she grabbed her coat. "I'll never get any work done. *Please* don't tell your parents I left. I hope you feel better but...oh my god, this is *disgusting*!"

Bizzy bolted out the door, and just like that, we were alone.

Heck grinned and high-fived me as we both farted again.

Flubflubflubflubflubflubflub.

It smelled like the butt-spray from a skunk who ate nothing but cabbage-kale-arugula smoothies.

"Now how do we make this stop?" I asked, pinching my nostrils shut.

"We can't," said Heck cheerfully. "We just have to wait until we run out of gas."

"I guess we'd better open some more windows," I said.

Then my phone vibrated with an incoming text from Detective Taylor.

We need to talk.

chapter 46

"DETECTIVE CLUB IS NOW IN SESSION," I ANNOUNCED, opening my notebook and clicking my pen.

Heck, Santos, and I were sitting at a corner table in the Elegant Grind. Santos had gotten out of school by calling and pretending to be his dad. It was easy, he told us: since Mr. Salgado was even more silent than his son, the secretary had no idea what either of their voices sounded like.

"Why can't we meet in your apartment?" asked Santos.

"It's being fumigated," Heck told him.

"Listen," I said. "Yesterday, Delores laid a trap for us. Now it's our turn to lay a trap for her. But we have to hurry, because Detective Taylor thinks we're at school, so we only have until the end of the day."

There was another reason we had to hurry: I really needed to pass gas again and I didn't want to do it inside the coffee shop, where everyone would know it was me.

"What kind of trap?" asked Santos.

"We'll wait outside her office and follow her. When she tries to poison someone, we'll use our phones to get the evidence Detective Taylor needs to close the case."

"Don't you think she'll just catch us again?" asked Heck.

"She thinks we're grounded, so she won't even be expecting us," I told him.

Santos looked like the words he was about to say were going to hurt his mouth, but he said them anyway: "Sometimes it's better to be afraid."

"What do you mean?" I asked.

"Because it makes you more careful," he said. "I think it will work better if we split up and hide."

After he explained, I realized Santos was right. His plan was better. Maybe he used all the time he saved by not talking to do extra thinking. Or maybe he kept quiet so he wouldn't have to let everybody know how smart he was. Either way, I was glad he was on our team.

When we left the coffee shop, Heck and I both farted so suddenly that Santos ran halfway down the block.

Back at the Arcanum, Heck stationed himself in a mop closet by the alley door in case Delores sneaked out the back. He had so many supplies in his backpack it was like he was going camping: a blanket and pillow, a gourmet picnic lunch, noise-canceling headphones, and his Nintendo Switch.

"Try not to get distracted," I warned him.

"Don't worry," he said. "If she gets past me, I'll just catch her on my skateboard."

Santos hid in a shadowy corner of the lounge, sinking deep into a leather chair where he could watch the lobby and the front door. Heck had given him a GoPro on a hand mount so he could record everything like a security camera.

"Don't get too comfortable and fall asleep," I cautioned Santos.

"I'm too nervous to sleep," he said.

I rode the elevator to the very top of the atrium. From the twelfth floor, I could see the doors to every apartment except the penthouse on the roof. When Delores came up in the elevator, I would know exactly where she got off and which apartment she entered.

Everyone ready? I texted our group chat. We had all put our phones on vibrate so nobody could hear us.

READY, Santos texted back immediately.

My brother didn't reply.

Heck, are you paying attention?? I texted.

He answered a little while later. **Sorry. Had to smash Wario.**

I didn't know how Heck could be so chill when I could hardly stop pacing. I circled the balcony, never taking my eyes off Delores's office door. It was time to put an end to her reign of terror.

My heart was pumping hard.

But I was prepared. I was psyched. I was ready to go.

I was...

chapter 47

I WAS...*BORED OUT OF MY MIND?!?*

In TV shows, detectives on stakeouts sit in their cars, drinking coffee and eating junk food until something exciting happens, but the boring parts are edited out.

So far, our stakeout was *only* the boring parts. Was this what Detective Taylor's job was really like?

The only good news was that I had finally stopped farting.

Well, mostly.

I had thought Delores would start her workday by poisoning someone right away, but so far, she hadn't come out of her office once. The most exciting thing I saw was the janitors cleaning up the lobby, which was still a mess from last night. I paced back and forth while they folded and stacked chairs and swept up discarded candles and crumpled flyers.

They left the pictures of Kermit, Serenity, Young-Jae, and Oskar on the table. Earlier that morning, I had seen that the glass in Kermit's picture frame had cracked when someone knocked it over. But the picture was still hanging in there—just like Kermit.

Have either of you seen anything? I texted the other two members of Detective Club.

Santos sent us a GIF of some comedian shaking his head: **NOPE.**

Heck sent a video file. I opened it up and pressed play. It started with a rat's-eye view of the alley—then Heck skated toward the phone's camera like he was determined to crush it with his trucks. At the last second, though, he ollied and jumped over.

Sick trick! texted Santos.

Aren't you supposed to be watching the back door? I texted.

It was hot in the closet, Heck wrote back. **But don't worry, I'll see her if she comes out. Anybody want to play Among Us?**

OK, answered Santos.

A quick game couldn't hurt, I supposed. I glanced down before writing my reply. What I saw nearly made me drop my phone off the balcony.

Delores was on the move!

chapter  48

Ducking down so Delores couldn't see me, I tracked her through the spaces in the railing of the twelfth-floor balcony.

She's out of her office, I texted. **Crossing the lobby.**

Headed where??? Heck wanted to know.

I didn't know. She walked toward the elevator...and then went right past it. When I realized her destination, I tapped out an update.

The bathroom. You'd better follow her, just to be sure.

The GIRLS' bathroom??? asked Heck.

Who, ME? asked Santos.

She might be mixing poison in the sink! I texted.

I have to give Santos credit, because he went after her. Leaving his hiding place, he sneaked across the atrium. Even though his face was as small as my fingernail, I could have sworn I saw him gulp.

He stopped at the women's restroom and put his ear against the door. Then he turned and ran away like his heels were on fire.

What happened?!? I texted.

He didn't answer.

Far below me, Delores stepped out of the bathroom and looked around suspiciously—then suddenly craned her neck and looked up.

I dropped out of sight and flattened myself on the floor. Did she know we were watching her again?

Finally, my phone vibrated.

I heard the flush, Santos texted. **I don't think she killed anybody in there, but she did do something really bad.**

WHAT? demanded Heck.

She didn't wash her hands.

WHAT KIND OF MONSTER DOESN'T WASH HER HANDS AFTER USING THE TOILET?!? demanded Heck, whose caps lock seemed stuck.

I didn't have time to answer because Delores was on the move again and I didn't want to lose her. I watched as she walked away from the bathroom, got on the elevator, and started riding it up.

I was out in the open, as easy to spot as a spider in a bathtub. She was going to see me if she came up to my floor. Just like a spider in a bathtub, I started running helplessly back and forth.

Fortunately, the elevator stopped on the tenth floor.

She was almost directly under me. I crawled to the other side of the balcony until she finally came into view. Delores DeWitt had stopped in front of apartment 1002.

Mr. Park's apartment.

Again.

Why did she keep returning to the scene of the crime?

Delores raised her huge key ring and turned it until she found the key she wanted. After looking both ways, she slotted it into the lock, went inside, and closed the door behind her.

I had been trying so hard to keep out of sight that I had completely forgotten to get any evidence.

She went into Mr. Park's apartment, I updated the group. **I'll get a picture of her coming out. Santos, make sure you get video of her coming down in the elevator and going back into her office.**

Santos texted a thumbs-up.

What about me? texted Heck.

Stay where you are and don't let her see you, I told him.

He sent the swearing emoji. I guess he was mad about being left out.

I rode the elevator down to ten and hid in an alcove just down the hall from Mr. Park's door. Sticking my phone around the corner so only the camera lens was showing, I started recording a video.

I watched the empty balcony on my screen for what seemed like forever.

And when Delores finally came out, I knew why she'd returned to the scene of the crime.

chapter 49

DELORES WAS CARRYING MR. PARK'S BEAUTIFUL BRONZE sculpture of Lady Justice. It looked *heavy*—she almost dropped it while she was locking the door—and it was probably worth a ton of money, too.

Lady Justice's blindfold meant she couldn't see who was stealing her. But I could. I kept recording video as Delores locked the door and lugged her loot back to the elevator.

She's coming down! I texted Santos and Heck.

I risked a look over the railing and saw Santos crouched behind a large potted plant, using his GoPro to get a perfect shot of Delores as she descended. He stood up for a better angle as she crossed the atrium and hurried toward her office.

But she didn't stop there. She kept going into the back hallway.

Coming your way, Heck! Santos texted.

As soon as Delores was out of sight, I rode the elevator back down. Santos met me at the bottom and we hurried after Delores. Heck wasn't in his closet. But the door leading to the alley was cracked open. Cautiously, we peeked out.

Delores was ten feet away and headed right for us!

I pulled the door closed, hoping she would think the wind had blown it shut. Her key scraped in the lock as we sprinted back down the hallway, through the atrium, all the way to the lounge, where we crouched behind a big leather couch. The new doorman never even looked up from the sports section of the *Chicago Sun-Times*.

"Where the heck did Heck go?" whispered Santos.

I had no idea, but a few minutes later, he rolled through the front door on his skateboard. I pulled him into the lounge so fast that his skateboard kept going without him.

"What happened?" I asked.

Heck was sweaty and excited. "Delores took that statue thingy outside into the alley, wrapped it in a blanket...and put it in the trunk of her car!"

"Please tell me you got it on video," I begged.

He tapped the GoPro strapped to his head. "Every second."

"Okay, let's check everyone's phones to make sure we got enough evidence," I said.

We sat down at the chess table and moved the pieces out of the way so we could watch our videos. Mine clearly showed Delores taking Lady Justice from Mr. Park's apartment.

Santos's captured her riding down the elevator and walking toward the back of the building.

Heck's caught her as she passed the janitor's closet and went out the back door. The camera glided as Heck skateboarded toward the door, then did a crazy somersault when he crashed and wrecked.

"I ran into a radiator," Heck explained. "Fortunately, my cast broke my fall."

On the video, he picked himself up, hurried outside, and hid behind a dumpster while Delores walked to her car. The statue was impossible to miss as she wrapped it up and stowed it in her trunk.

"I got locked out when she went back inside, which is why I had to go around the building," explained Heck. "But now we have a perfect chain of evidence."

"She's poisoning people just so she can steal from them?" asked Santos.

"I guess so," I said. "When the police check her phone and computer, they're going to find out that she's selling the stuff on eBay and Etsy."

"This is so sad," said Santos.

"Definitely," agreed Heck.

"But the good news is, we just ended her criminal career," I said.

Then we heard Delores's voice behind us. "There they are, the little creeps. Arrest them, officer!"

chapter 50

DETECTIVE TAYLOR AND DELORES WERE STANDING IN the lounge entrance. We had been so busy watching the videos that we hadn't even noticed them. But I did notice that Detective Taylor's tie looked like fruit salad that had been smashed with a sledge-hammer.

"These are the criminal children I reported last night," Delores told him. "I was performing a routine check on unit 1002 when I caught them trying to break in."

Detective Taylor's expression was hard to read. I wanted to believe he was as disgusted with Delores as I was. But it looked more like he was disappointed in us.

"Why aren't you kids in school?" he asked.

Delores butted in, happy we'd also been busted for skipping. "They're probably planning to break into more apartments. And why not, since their lazy teachers and clueless guardians have no idea where they are?"

She didn't know we had followed her this time, so I just let her run her mouth. It was only going to be sweeter when I turned around and dunked on her.

"It's true that we should be in school," I confessed as Delores grinned with delight. "It's also true that Heck and I went to Mr. Park's apartment last night. It's so full of fascinating, valuable antiques that it's almost irresistible."

Heck and Santos were looking at me like I had lost my mind. And if Delores had been any happier, she probably would have exploded. She obviously expected us to get arrested while she got away with her crimes.

She had no idea she was facing checkmate.

"Are you saying Delores is telling the truth?" asked Detective Taylor, looking almost sick.

I shook my head. "It's been driving us crazy, trying to figure out why Delores would hurt nice people like Kermit, Serenity, Oskar, and Young-Jae. Like you said, Detective Taylor: *What's her motive?* But now we know."

Delores turned white, then gray, then green as, one by one, we took out our screens to show Detective Taylor the videos.

And one by one, we pressed play.

chapter 51

DELORES'S EXPRESSION WHEN DETECTIVE TAYLOR snapped the handcuffs around her wrists chilled me to the bone. If looks could kill, I would have been one more body in the morgue.

"You won't get away with this!" she ranted. "You have no idea who you're messing with, you little freaks! I'LL MAKE YOU PAY!"

She lunged at me, getting so close I could see specks of food in the cracks of her yellowing teeth. But just as she whipped her neck forward and tried to headbutt me, Detective Taylor caught her by the shoulders and pulled her back.

"Try not to make things any worse for yourself," he told her.

"Actually, go ahead," I said, even though my heart was pounding so hard it was hurting my ribs.

Delores had gone full werewolf in broad daylight. Her eyes were wild and her hair was practically standing on end as she wrestled with Detective Taylor.

Finally, twisting her arm, he turned her around and marched her toward the front door.

"Come on, I'm going to need to take your statements, too," he told us.

We got into the back of Detective Taylor's car while he buckled Delores into the passenger seat with her hands cuffed behind her back. Santos seemed nervous to be sitting behind her, especially because she kept turning her head to spray us with saliva.

"When all this is over, you're going to wish you'd never been BORN!" she screeched.

Heck started taking pictures of her with ugly Snapchat filters and showing them to her.

"One of these will make the perfect mug shot," he told her.

That shut her up.

At the police station, Detective Taylor told us to wait at his desk while he took Delores through a door labeled INTERROGATION.

"Can I watch?" I asked.

He shook his head. "Sorry, Minerva, but I don't want to have to explain to a judge how I let a twelve-year-old play bad cop while we got a suspect to confess. We need to make sure this holds up in court."

I had my hands full keeping Heck out of trouble, anyway. He had found Detective Taylor's pepper spray and was planning to invent a new snack with a bag of chips he had bought from the vending machine.

"I'll call them Cop Shop Flaming Hots," said Heck, popping the bag open and getting ready to spritz them with something that should only be used for self-defense.

"Are you crazy?" I asked, grabbing the canister out of his hand and throwing it into Detective Taylor's desk drawer. "First Molotov cocktails and now pepper spray. I have no idea how you survived until the fifth grade."

Heck shoved a chip into his mouth and crunched it unhappily. "This is seriously lacking in flavor."

Santos came over. "That guy over there says he'll show us some magic tricks," he told us.

I looked up. "That guy" was Amazing Andy, who had apparently already been arrested again. His tuxedo was torn and frayed but he was looking at us like a dog hoping for a treat.

"Don't stand too close unless you want your pockets emptied," I warned them as they eagerly rushed over for a show. I decided to skip it.

Detective Taylor was gone for a long time. I figured it was just taking him a while to write down all the details from Delores's murder confessions. Maybe she had poisoned more than the four people we knew about. If she was doing it in the building where she lived, too, maybe we had even stopped the worst poisoner in Chicago. Maybe the world.

When he finally came back to the detectives' room, I expected him to be grinning from ear to ear because we'd closed the case. But he didn't look happy.

"Well, she confessed to stealing," he said. "But she *insists* she didn't murder anyone."

"She's guilty!" I said. "She has to be!"

Detective Taylor slumped into his chair. "We found the statue in her car, just like you said. And in her home, my team found valuable items that belonged to Kermit and Serenity. Her internet history shows she was an active seller on e-commerce sites."

"Well, there you go," I said.

He shook his head. "But we haven't found any trace of the poisons she used. I can charge her for theft, but I still don't have a single piece of evidence that she's a murderer."

chapter 52

I COULDN'T BELIEVE WHAT I WAS HEARING. I SAT DOWN in the chair next to Detective Taylor's desk and looked up at his weary face. He seemed just as frustrated as I was.

"But she went into their homes after they were poisoned and stole stuff!" I said. "Isn't that proof?"

"It definitely looks bad for her," he said. "But she claims she stole from them only because they *happened* to be poisoned. We haven't had time to see if anything's missing from Oskar's apartment, but I'd be surprised if there is, since he didn't live in the building and she doesn't have his key."

"What if she killed Oskar because he figured out what she was doing?" I asked.

"It's possible," Detective Taylor admitted.

"And if nobody else gets poisoned while she's locked up here, doesn't that prove she did it?"

"Not necessarily," said Detective Taylor. "If the real culprit knows Delores is under suspicion, they might stop in order to make her look more guilty. Or not. It's also possible there are other victims we don't know about behind closed doors."

That thought made my skin feel all prickly. If Serenity hadn't made it to the elevator before collapsing, nobody would have even known she was poisoned. Lots of our neighbors lived alone.

"Shouldn't we check on everyone in the building?" I asked. "Just to make sure they're okay?"

Detective Taylor nodded. "You're right. Let's do it."

Just then, Heck and Santos come back, looking very proud of themselves.

"That guy over there just showed us the coolest trick," said Santos.

"How to escape from handcuffs!" said Heck, holding them up. "He gave them to us as a souvenir."

We all turned to look: Amazing Andy was gone.

"Where is he?" asked Detective Taylor.

"He said he had to go to a birthday party," said Heck.

"Wait here," said Detective Taylor as he jumped up and ran out of the room.

"Oh no," said Santos, who seemed to have finally realized what had just happened.

Disgusted, I rolled my eyes at the other members of Detective Club. "You guys do realize that we're trying to *catch* criminals, not let them go, right?"

chapter  53

LIGHTS WERE GLOWING IN THE WINDOWS OF THE ARCA-num by the time we finally got back from the police station. It had taken Detective Taylor almost an hour to catch Amazing Andy. As we climbed out of his car onto the sidewalk, a chilly breeze rattled the dead leaves in the gutter.

"My team is still tied up searching Delores's house," he told us. "Do you want to help me knock on doors?"

"Just try and stop me," I said, while Heck nodded in agreement.

Detective Taylor showed his badge to the replacement doorman and we headed inside.

"This is what police call a wellness check," he explained to us. "All we're doing is checking to see if anyone needs help."

"What if there's no answer?" I asked.

"Write down the apartment number so I can go in using Delores's keys if necessary," said Detective Taylor. "But some people just might not be home from work yet. Or they could be out of town."

"Got it," said Heck.

Detective Taylor craned his neck as he counted the balconies rising above us. "We'll cover more ground if we split up into two teams. Minerva, you and Santos take the even-numbered floors, and Heck and I will take odd-numbered ones."

I was so eager to get started that I was practically running in place. "What are we waiting for?"

"I could use more detectives like you," he said, grinning at me.

Santos and I got off the elevator on two, and Heck and Detective Taylor rode up to three. We worked fast, knocking on doors and writing down what happened before moving on. On a new page in my notebook, I had listed the apartment numbers, followed by columns labeled NO PROBLEM! and NO ANSWER!

Of the eight units on the second floor, five people answered the door, looked at us funny, and told us everything was fine. I marked those *no problem.* Only two were *no answer.* The remaining one was our own apartment.

I decided to check and see if Bizzy had gotten back from the University of Chicago yet. If she had, I needed to tell her why Heck and I weren't home like we were supposed to be. She would have to tell our parents, but Delores's arrest meant we probably wouldn't get in trouble.

"Don't you have a key?" Santos asked as I knocked on the door.

"Yes, but I don't want to startle her," I told him.

When Bizzy didn't answer, I turned to go, thinking she was probably still at school.

Santos stopped me. "Wait a minute. I heard something."

For a moment, all I could hear was Heck and Detective Taylor knocking on doors above us.

Then there was a soft sliding sound, like socks on a hardwood floor. Followed by a BUMP.

I dug in my pocket for the key and opened the door.

The lights weren't on, so it took me a few seconds to see Bizzy feeling her way along the wall toward us.

"Bizzy?" I asked. "Are you all right?"

As she got closer, I could hear her gasping for breath. I sniffed, just to make sure she wasn't still gagging from our gas attack—but the open windows had done their job and cleared the air.

"What's wrong?" I asked as I switched on the light.

Bizzy looked at me with eyes wide from terror. She tried to say something but it was like her throat was clogged. Her voice was a strangled hiss.

"Poison," she gasped. *"Poison!"*

chapter 54

EVERYTHING HAPPENED SO FAST AFTER THAT. BIZZY collapsed. I screamed for help. Santos fainted. Or maybe Santos screamed for help and *I* fainted—it was kind of a blur. Detective Taylor got there so quickly I think he must have climbed down from the balcony.

Now that I think about it, it was Santos who fainted, not me, but the whole thing felt so unreal I could hardly believe it was happening. I did chest compressions on Bizzy while Detective Taylor called for help on his police radio.

I guess that worked even faster than calling 911, because Big Joan and Little John got there before

I finished singing "Rumor Has It" in my head. (I *think* it was in my head.)

"You're getting pretty good at this, Minerva," Big Joan told me as she took over.

"I don't *want* to have to be good at this," I told her.

Little John woke up Santos with smelling salts again and then put an oxygen bag on Bizzy. The teddy bear tattoo on his bicep bulged as he helped Big Joan lift the gurney.

The next thing I knew, Heck, Santos, and I were in the back seat of Detective Taylor's car again. This time we held on for dear life as he weaved through traffic, following the smoking tires of the ambulance toward DuSable Hospital.

"Man, she's fast," said Detective Taylor with a whistle, admiring Big Joan's driving.

Through the windows in the ambulance's back doors, I could see Little John squeezing the oxygen bag to keep Bizzy alive. He must have strapped her down tightly, because the stretcher didn't budge, even when Big Joan made the boxy ambulance drift around a corner like she was in *The Fast and the Furious*.

For some reason, all I could think about was Disney World—and not just because I would rather have been in the Magic Kingdom than in Chicago. The day I had spent there with my cousin was my favorite memory of all time.

Not because she had spent fifteen minutes talking to Woody from *Toy Story* without realizing he was seven feet tall and made out of foam. ("How was I supposed to know he wasn't a real cowboy?" she said after I clued her in.)

And not because she crossed the street, got caught in the Disney World parade, and just...kept going.

And it wasn't even because when we were boarding Splash Mountain, she somehow didn't get a seat, and went through the whole ride sitting on *top* of the giant log.

Only my cousin could be the real source of amusement at an amusement park.

The *real* reason that day was my favorite was because I dropped my ice cream in some horse poop.

Well, not *that*, but what happened afterward. A horse pulling a trolley had just dropped a steaming load of doo-doo on Main Street, USA. And before the guy with the broom could sweep it up, my melting ball of ice cream chose that exact spot to swan dive off my cone.

Bizzy didn't laugh. She didn't even hesitate.

"Want mine?" she said, even though she hadn't taken a lick.

Because she's basically one of the nicest people in the whole world.

"Is Bizzy going to be okay?" I practically whispered as the hospital came into view. I was almost afraid to say it out loud because I was afraid of the answer.

Detective Taylor didn't say anything.

He didn't know, either.

chapter 55

Detective Taylor took charge at the ER, hurrying over to the intake nurse while Big Joan and Little John rolled Bizzy inside. But from the way he was shaking his head, I could tell he didn't like what she was saying.

I moved closer so I could hear, and Heck and Santos came with me.

Then Detective Taylor pointed at us.

"These kids are her cousins," he told the nurse. "And I'll be damned if I'm going to let her become another body in the morgue. So I want you to go back there and find a bed for her *now!*"

"Yes, sir." The nurse gulped before hurrying away.

"Detective Taylor's a tough guy," whispered Heck.

"I'm glad he's *our* tough guy," I whispered back.

Detective Taylor walked over to us.

"She said they were full up, but she'll find something," he said. "That's the good news."

"What's the bad news?" I asked.

"She also told me that Young-Jae Park didn't make it."

That made three victims. Santos and I hadn't saved him after all.

"We tried our best," I told Santos, feeling sick to my stomach.

Moments later, the nurse returned with a doctor and an orderly. We all watched as they rushed Bizzy into an area labeled HOSPITAL STAFF ONLY.

Detective Taylor's cell phone rang and he moved away to take the call. When he came back, he looked like he'd heard some encouraging news.

"As soon as I can get more officers to help, I'm going to go back to the Arcanum and we're going to pound on every single door until we're sure everyone is safe," he said. "But first I have to go talk to some people who might have some important information. I'll be in touch."

He hurried out to his car, leaving us alone in the waiting room.

"Now that your babysitter is in the hospital, who's looking after you?" asked Santos.

"She's not our *babysitter*," I told him. "We can look after ourselves."

"We should tell Mom and Dad, though," said Heck.

He was right. I called them on FaceTime. When they answered, their phone was bouncing around so much it took me a second to see that Dad was driving a speedboat, bumping up and down on the waves. He and Mom were both wearing wetsuits and scuba gear with big knives strapped to their belts.

"We're kind of busy at the moment, Minerva," said Dad.

I could hardly hear him because of the wind whipping past his phone.

"Bizzy's in the hospital!" I shouted. "We think she's been poisoned!"

Mom and Dad looked at each other. Dad was probably wondering how someone from our own family could have gotten hurt when there was such a statistically small chance of it happening.

But for once, he said something I wanted to hear.

As he turned the wheel of the boat sharply, heading back to shore, he said, "We'll be there as soon as we can. Unfortunately, it's going to take at least thirty-six hours before we can get to Chicago."

"I'll call Aunt Arabella and tell her about Bizzy," said Mom. "Stay safe."

"I want to," I told her. "But how?"

Obviously, nobody knew the answer to that.

"You'll figure it out," said Dad.

chapter 56

HECK, SANTOS, AND I STOOD AT THE FOOT OF KERMIT'S bed. He didn't look any better, but at least he didn't look any worse. The flowers I had brought him on Sunday were wilting, and to be totally honest, the room smelled like sour feet.

"This is your friend?" asked Santos. "He's so...*old*."

"We're chess friends," I explained. "It's not like we hang out at the mall."

"If *he's* still alive, then there's hope for Bizzy, right?" said Heck hopefully.

We still hadn't gotten an update on our cousin's condition, but I was tired of sitting in the ER waiting room, so I figured we might as well check in on

Kermit. Nurse Rosamie told us she still hadn't seen him open his eyes.

If only Kermit and Bizzy could tell us how they'd been poisoned.

My eyes were getting blurry again with tears. The whole thing was hopeless. Kermit wasn't getting any better and Bizzy could die if Detective Taylor didn't find out more about the poison soon. Too many people had died already.

I wanted to throw something—and the chessboard was the easiest thing to throw. Before I could get there, Santos stepped in front of me.

"Who's playing?" he asked.

"I am, but I don't know why I bother. Kermit's moves just don't make any sense."

"This *game* doesn't make sense," said Heck.

Santos studied the positions of the pieces. "Who's playing white?"

"I am," I told him. "Kermit was trying to trick me into an easy checkmate, which he should have known would never work, because I'm too good to fall for it."

"Maybe you should take another look," said Santos.

I wiped my eyes. After I'd brought a second pawn into the middle to break up Kermit's attack, he had moved his queen over to the other side of the board. Now both his queen and his bishop were threatening the space in front of my king.

And I hadn't even seen it coming.

"He's beating you!" said Heck, starting to laugh.

"The game's not over yet," I said.

But it was true. Kermit had distracted me by making me think he was going to do one thing, when the whole time, he was planning another line of attack.

I was so happy, I couldn't even be mad that he'd tricked me. I started laughing, too.

Kermit knew exactly what he was doing.

He had been laying a trap.

chapter 57

"STOP IT, MINERVA!" SAID HECK. "WHAT ARE YOU *doing?*"

It had been so long since we'd gotten any good news that my arms had acted on their own and wrapped Heck in a big hug—and now he was fighting to get away from me.

I didn't like it any more than he did, so I was happy to let him go. Right away he started trying to wipe off any germs I might have given him.

"That was an accident," I told him.

"You HATE losing," Heck said. "You hate it so much that nobody in the family will even play games with you. If Kermit's winning, why are you in such a good mood?"

I punched him in the shoulder to officially cancel the hug.

"I'm happy because Kermit's getting better, you dope," I said. "And now that I know what he's doing, don't assume I'm going to lose."

"Since he's still sick, maybe you should just let him win?" suggested Santos.

"I'm not *that* happy," I told him.

As we headed back down to the ER to check on Bizzy, I replayed Kermit's moves again in my mind. They reminded me of something I had seen before on YouTube. There are tons of YouTubers who post cool chess videos, and I was pretty sure the pattern was one with an awesome name, like the Fried Liver Attack, the Queen's Gambit, or the Sicilian Defense.

But what was it?

The ER waiting room was so full we could hardly squeeze back in. Outside the sliding doors, a line of ambulances was backed up into the parking lot, their flashers making a red-and-white lightning storm as they waited to unload new patients.

A TV on the wall showed a reporter standing in front of a messy accident on the expressway.

"Imagine the world's largest science-fair experiment taking place on one of the nation's busiest highways," said the reporter, whose name was Sunny Rhodes. "That's exactly what happened here tonight, when a tanker filled with vinegar crashed into a trailer truck filled with baking soda. The volcanic eruption caused a fifty-two-car pileup that is currently overwhelming local hospitals."

"So *that's* what happened," said Heck. "I wish *I'd* been driving one of those trucks!"

When Heck got old enough to drive, I planned to stay off the streets—*permanently.*

"Stay here while I find out about Bizzy," I told Heck and Santos.

I had to fight my way through the crowd and yell before I finally got the nurse's attention. She told me that Bizzy had been moved to intensive care and we wouldn't be able to visit her until morning.

Where are you? I texted Detective Taylor.

Trying to get answers on the toxins, he wrote. **Meeting with the medical examiner and the poison center. Will update you when I get back to my desk.**

When I crossed the room again, Heck was still watching TV and Santos was falling asleep.

"We need to go to the police station to wait for Detective Taylor," I said. "Sitting around and checking my phone for texts isn't going to help Bizzy get better."

Santos yawned. "I should go home. It's super late and I need to find out how much homework I missed."

I seriously could not believe what I was hearing.

"Would you rather do homework or *solve a mystery*?" I asked him. "Not only will we save lives and catch a killer, who knows, we might even be famous!"

"Being famous would make me so nervous that I would pass out every day, before I even got out of bed in the morning," said Santos with a shudder. "Besides, how would we even get to the police station from here?"

"I'll get us a cab," said Heck, finally tearing his eyes away from the disaster on the TV screen. "I still have *lots* of cookie money."

chapter 58

THE POLICE STATION WAS JUST AS CROWDED AND CRAZY as the hospital.

We walked through the front doors and were immediately caught in the middle of a bunch of people who were pushing and shoving one another and yelling at the two officers behind the desk. Someone was playing loud music on a Bluetooth speaker like it was some kind of weird dance party.

Then two cops brought in a man and a woman who were struggling to throw punches at each other.

"I didn't steal your ring!" shouted the man.

"So you think *I* put it in your pocket?" the woman shouted right back.

"Is Chicago always like this at night?" Santos asked after thcy had passed us.

"I don't know," I told him. "I'm never out this late, either."

Detective Taylor still wasn't answering his texts. But one of the desk officers recognized me and told me we could wait for him in the detectives' room.

As we walked past INTERROGATION, I saw a window in the wall. And through the window, I saw that a miserable-looking Delores was still sitting inside.

"Look!" I told Heck and Santos.

When Santos saw Delores, he dropped down below the window.

"Don't worry, it's a two-way mirror," I explained. "We can see her, but she can't see us."

"I'll make sure," said Heck.

Walking closer to the glass, he made a face at her. And not just any face: his freakiest face. He turned his eyelids inside out, stretched his cheeks with his pinkies, and made a pig nose with his index fingers—but Delores just stared blankly into space.

I pulled on the door but it didn't open.

"What's *wrong* with you?" asked Santos. "Why are you trying to get in?"

"I want to talk to her," I explained. "I was thinking about it on the way over, and I finally realized Delores is right: She can't be the killer."

"But she stole the statue!" said Heck.

"She's a thief for sure," I agreed. "But we watched her all day and she didn't break into our apartment. So how could she have poisoned Bizzy?"

"Maybe with some kind of timed-release pill?" suggested Santos.

I looked at Delores. She was aiming one of her ears at the window. She couldn't see us, but maybe she had heard us.

"Then why weren't we poisoned, too?" I said, lowering my voice. "I just don't think she's guilty. But maybe she knows something that can help."

"If she didn't do it, wouldn't she have already told Detective Taylor everything, so she could prove she's innocent?" asked Santos.

That was an excellent argument, and Detective Taylor obviously had more experience as a detective than me. But I also knew the Arcanum better than he did.

"Maybe he didn't ask her the right question," I told Santos.

"It doesn't matter anyway, because this door is locked and we don't have a key," said Heck.

I pulled on the door handle again. Still locked. I looked through the glass at Delores. Still ugly. I scanned the detectives' room...*Amazing Andy was still there.*

"Ta-da!" I said.

I led them over to the magician. Detective Taylor obviously hadn't had time to deal with him, either. Amazing Andy had fallen asleep, even though both of his hands were now handcuffed to the arms of his chair so he couldn't escape. Drool oozed from the corner of his open mouth.

When I poked him, his eyes popped open.

"I'm Minerva, and these guys are Heck and Santos," I told him.

"We've met," he said, eyeing us suspiciously. "What do you want?"

I felt like a magician revealing a trick of my own when I asked: "How would you like to help us catch a murderer?"

CASE FILES

Name: Amazing Andy AKA Gern Blanston

Occupation: Magician

Relationship to case: Keeps showing up at the police station

Hair: Black but turning gray

Eyes: Sad, like a hound dog staring at your hamburger

Age: 37. (I asked and he told me.)

Identifying characteristics: ALWAYS wears a tuxedo. (Probably doesn't own any other clothes.) Carries everything he owns in his pockets. (Has a LOT of pockets.)

Personality: Dishonest. And depressed. (Probably wishes he had a TV show instead of performing at birthday parties.)

Habits, behavior & special talents: Really good at picking locks!

DETECTIVE'S NOTES:

Amazing Andy would probably be Chicago's most popular birthday-party magician if he could just stop stealing the birthday presents.

After all, he's really good at escaping, and kids would love watching him escape from handcuffs and a straitjacket inside a truck that's wrapped with chains.

Unfortunately, he does everything backward: He locks up the birthday boy or girl...along with all their friends...and the parents...and then disappears with the presents!

So you can see the problem.

I still think he basically has a good heart. (If he didn't make that disappear, too.)

chapter 59

A<small>MAZING</small> A<small>NDY LOOKED AT ME LIKE</small> I <small>HAD JUST ASKED</small> him to fly to the moon with a helium balloon.

"Look, kid, I'm already in enough trouble over that misunderstanding with the birthday party," he said. "I can't afford to get mixed up in a murder."

"Detective Taylor said it was more than one birthday party," I told him.

"And you were *stealing*," added Heck.

Amazing Andy stuck out his lower lip and pouted. "I deserved a tip for putting on a good show."

His tuxedo was so wrinkled and worn I figured he probably slept in it. Did he own any other clothes? Did he even have a place to live? I guess those were things he couldn't make magically appear.

"I just need you to pick a lock so I can talk to somebody," I said. "Will you help us?"

"What's in it for me?" he asked.

"If I'm right and we solve the case, I'll tell Detective Taylor," I said. "He can ask the judge to give you a break."

Amazing Andy shook his head. "I've known Detective Taylor for a long time, and he'll never go for it."

"Then I'll hire you for my next birthday party!" said Heck. He added, "As long as you promise not to steal anything."

"And you also have to promise not to try to escape," I warned him.

"Where do you live?" asked Amazing Andy.

"The Arcanum, on North Dearborn Parkway," Heck said.

The magician whistled. "Nice building. Okay, I promise. I'll pick the lock."

Actually, he had to pick *three* locks—starting with his own handcuffs. Amazing Andy asked for two big metal paperclips, which I found in the top drawer of Detective Taylor's desk. After bending one according to Amazing Andy's instructions, I handed it over and watched as he went to work.

"You know, you'd make a good magician's assistant," he said, curling his wrist and twisting the paperclip in one of the handcuffs' keyholes.

"Thanks, but I'm already an assistant detective," I told him.

Amazing Andy really was an escape artist—it didn't take him long to open both sets of handcuffs. The open ends were still dangling from his wrists as we hurried back to INTERROGATION.

"I don't want anything to do with this," Santos said. He leaned against Detective Taylor's desk while we ran off.

At the door to Delores's temporary cell, Heck and I watched as Amazing Andy crouched down and worked both paperclips into the lock. Within thirty seconds, I heard a *click* as the lock released.

Amazing Andy looked up and grinned. "Open sesame!"

As Heck escorted him back to his chair, I took a deep breath and stepped in front of the door.

The last time I'd seen Delores, she had tried to headbutt me. She never would have gotten arrested if it wasn't for me, and she knew it.

Without Detective Taylor to stop her, what would she try this time?

chapter 60

WHEN I WALKED INTO THE ROOM, THE FIRST THING out of my mouth was a burp so loud that I covered my ears just in case it happened again.

This was *not* how I planned to start the interrogation. But I couldn't help it. Facing Delores one-on-one in the tiny room made me more nervous than anything that had happened so far. I was going to have to squeeze my brain like a sponge and use every last ounce of my smarts if I was going to outwit her.

"Where's Detective Taylor?" she asked.

"He's in a meeting, learning about the poisons used on Kermit, Serenity, Oskar, and Mr. Park," I said. *And Bizzy*, I thought sadly. Delores wouldn't know there had been another poisoning.

"And he sent a twelve-year-old *girl* to talk to me?" asked Delores, sneering. "What a joke! Chicago must really be falling apart if the police department is recruiting spoiled brats like you."

"I came on my own," I admitted.

When Delores stood up from behind the metal table, I saw that she wasn't even wearing handcuffs. In three quick steps she was at the door.

"So if I decide to just walk out of here, there's no one to stop me," she said, with an evil gleam in her eyes.

"You could probably make it all the way out of the station, and I'd get in trouble for letting you go," I told her.

"Keep talking, because I like what I'm hearing," said Delores.

My skin felt itchy. Now that she was behind me, her hands were uncomfortably close to my neck. But when I moved over to the opposite side of the table, I felt like *I* was the one being interrogated....

Another nervous burp bubbled its way up before I could swallow it down, but I forced myself to shrug.

"I didn't think you were so dumb that you'd actually *leave*," I told her. "If you want to, go ahead."

Delores looked at the door. Then she looked at me. For once, she seemed unsure of herself.

"What do you mean?" she asked.

"You said you were innocent, but if you leave, you'll only look guilty," I said. "If you stay and help me find the real killer, you'll be a lot better off. You'll still lose your job for stealing, of course. But maybe you can get out of going to jail."

Delores leaned over the table toward me. "Listen, you little monster. All I know is that you pop up every time someone at the Arcanum falls over. *You* should be Detective Taylor's top suspect, not me."

I wasn't tall enough to headbutt Delores, but I leaned closer anyway, because now I was getting mad. Maybe I could at least give her a bloody lip.

"My cousin Bizzy was poisoned tonight," I told her. "And if you think I had anything to do with that, you are out of your messed-up mind!"

Delores rolled her eyes so far back in her head I was surprised they didn't turn a full circle.

Apparently, she didn't think you couldn't poison someone just because they were a part of your family.

"No one else knew more about what happened in the building than you and Oskar," I continued. "And now Oskar can't tell us anything. Isn't there *anyone* you suspect besides me?"

"Nope," said Delores, shaking her head.

"What about other victims?" I asked. "Are there any people you haven't seen for a long time, who seem to have disappeared?"

"Your parents," she said smugly.

"They'll be here soon enough," I told her. *"Think."*

She frowned, like she was actually thinking about it—and then her eyebrows went up in surprise, like she had really remembered something. But she didn't *say* anything. A moment later, her face had settled into its usual sneer.

"Tell me what you know," I said.

"I'm sure it's nothing," said Delores.

"I'll be the judge of that. Just stop wasting time!"

She sighed, like saying her next words was going to be an exhausting chore. "Lothar and Ursula Ernst, who live in the penthouse—I haven't seen them for weeks. They're probably just on vacation. But most residents fill out a form if they're going away for a long time, and they never did."

"I'll check it out," I said, squeezing past her to freedom.

Delores eyed the open door. She was still thinking about making a break for it.

I slammed it hard, locking it, before she could try.

chapter 61

WERE LOTHAR AND URSULA ERNST THE FIRST VICTIMS of the poisoner...*or were they the ones doing the poisoning?*

Either way, this new clue just had to be important. As I walked back through the empty detectives' room, I texted Detective Taylor.

I found out something that could be a **REALLY BIG DEAL**, I wrote. When will you be back at the station?

He didn't answer. I sure hoped his meeting would be worth it.

Heck and Santos were watching Amazing Andy do card tricks on Detective Taylor's desk.

"Put his handcuffs back on," I told them. "We need to go."

"I called my dad and he said you guys can stay at my place until your parents get home," Santos told me.

"That's great," I said. "We can go there as soon as we follow the new lead Delores gave me."

"But it's almost midnight," he groaned.

"I'll get us another cab!" said Heck, charging out of the room.

I made sure the handcuffs were locked around Amazing Andy's wrists. Then I tore a piece of paper out of my notebook and started writing a message to Detective Taylor.

"We're going to the Arcanum penthouse," I wrote. "The people who live there haven't been seen for a LONG time!"

After looking at the unhappy magician in the wrinkled tuxedo, I added: "P.S. Amazing Andy has been very helpful."

I figured it couldn't hurt. I left the note on Detective Taylor's desk.

"Good luck," said Amazing Andy.

"Thanks," I said. "Good luck to you, too."

As we walked past the two-way mirror on our way out, I stuck out my tongue at Delores. Santos did the same thing.

If he was finally getting braver, now was the perfect time.

chapter 62

WE STEPPED OUT OF THE ELEVATOR INTO A LOBBY WITH a black-and-white chessboard floor, green velvet curtains, and a table holding a vase of colorful peacock feathers. Across from us was the door to the penthouse.

The elevator button was labeled PH, but this was actually the thirteenth floor of the Arcanum. In all of human history, has thirteen *ever* been a lucky number?

I lifted the heavy door knocker and slammed it down three times. The knocks were as loud as gunshots, but nobody answered.

And of course the door was locked.

Santos turned to leave. "I guess we'd better go to my house."

"Wait," said Heck. "Look up there! I think I can make it through."

Over the door, the transom window was hanging open.

He set the vase of feathers down on the floor while Santos and I moved the table over to the door. When Heck climbed on top of it, the whole thing wobbled like it couldn't wait to collapse. Fortunately, it didn't, but even standing on his tiptoes, Heck couldn't reach high enough.

"Someone give me a boost," he demanded.

"I nominate Santos," I said. "He's the tallest *and* the strongest."

Looking seasick, Santos got up and balanced on the table like he was surfing in a flat pond but expected a tidal wave to wipe him out any second. Then he laced his fingers together and lifted Heck's foot until Heck could scramble through the opening.

As soon as my brother's feet disappeared, we

heard a CRASH like a cannonball destroying a china cabinet.

Then a THUD like the cannonball had just landed on the floor.

Then a YOWL like a cat whose tail got pulled— but that was Heck, too.

"I'm okay!" he yelled a moment later.

Then the door swung open.

The Ernsts obviously had tons of money because their apartment looked like a mansion—but their interior decorator must have died a hundred years ago. The entryway was carpeted with leopard and zebra skins, below an elephant's-foot ottoman and a chair made out of ivory tusks.

"Cool!" said Heck.

"Gross," said Santos.

"You know, I'm pretty sure everything in this room is illegal," I said.

The rest of the place had the exact same theme. Jungle plants grew toward a skylight in the living room, which was as big as a basketball court. Its walls were lined with masks, shields, spears, and other stuff that should have been in a museum.

"Delores would love to get her hands on all of this," I said as we walked into a library filled with leather-bound books. "She could be the world's first eBay billionaire."

Then I opened a set of sliding doors.

We froze.

And I finally understood what Kermit had been trying to tell me all along.

chapter 63

THE HUGE, DARK ROOM WAS FILLED WITH DOZENS OF glowing glass cages, or vivariums, the kind you would find in a pet store. But this wasn't a pet store.

In a pet store, you can expect to find animals like gerbils, hamsters, and guinea pigs. I don't like any of those rodents because they remind me too much of rats. But even I have to admit that the worst thing gerbils, hamsters, and guinea pigs can do is pee in your hand.

The caged creatures in the Ernsts' creepy apartment could do a lot worse than that.

They could kill you, for starters.

"Guys? I have an extremely bad feeling about this," said Santos.

"Me, too," I said. "But we can't turn back now."

As we crept slowly into the room, we saw frogs, lizards, snakes, spiders, and scorpions sitting patiently behind glass. It was like they were all just waiting for someone stupid enough to put a hand inside and try to pick them up.

In the vivarium nearest me, a hideous scorpion arched its tail over its head. I could see the swollen sac of venom just behind its stinger.

"*Hottentotta tamulus*," I read from a card. "Commonly known as the Indian red scorpion. Most venomous scorpion in the world."

"Check this out!" said Heck, running ahead to the next case. "*Oxyuranus scutellatus*, coastal taipan snake. This one is the most dangerous snake on the continent of Australia!"

The reddish-brown snake suddenly launched itself forward and smacked into the glass, making Heck jump back. He laughed nervously—after checking himself for bite marks.

"G-golden p-poison f-frog," stammered Santos, reading another label. "*Phyllobates terribilis*. It looks like the f-frog we saw in the b-basement."

Lothar and Ursula Ernst were collectors. And they didn't collect coins, comic books, or Pokémon like normal people. No, they had gathered all of the world's most poisonous animals to create the deadliest zoo that ever existed.

"Kermit wasn't just trying to win the chess game," I said.

"Seriously?" groaned Heck. "All you ever think about is chess."

"Don't you get it?" I said. "He was sending me a message! He was playing the Spider Attack... *because he was bitten by a spider.*"

Heck and Santos looked at me with eyes as big and round as ping-pong balls.

Many of the vivariums contained spiders. Even though they were behind glass, I didn't want to get too close, because I hate spiders just as much as I hate rats.

But for some reason I had to look. I couldn't help myself.

As I moved closer, I saw black widows, brown recluses, and yellow sac spiders. According to the cards on their cages, all of them carried lethal amounts of venom.

Then I saw a card that read, *"Phoneutria,* or Brazilian wandering spider." This vivarium was open...*and empty.*

I felt a tickle on my neck.

"Get it off! Get it off! GET IT OFF!" I screamed while I spun around, flapping my arms and trying to wriggle out of my skin.

Santos grabbed me. Heck looked at my neck....

And started *laughing.*

"It's just your own hair, Minerva!" he cackled.

"How was I supposed to know?" I said, as I broke free from Santos.

But my skin was still crawling. Because the Brazilian wandering spider was out there somewhere.

Where had it wandered off to?

chapter 64

"HOW DO YOU THINK IT GOT OUT?" WHISPERED HECK.

After I showed him the card and the open cage, he had suddenly started taking the escaped arachnid more seriously.

"I don't know," I whispered back. "But once it got out, it could go anywhere in the building using the speaking tubes and the air vents..."

"Not to mention the garbage chutes and transoms," he added.

"...all the way into our apartment...where it bit Bizzy!" I said, shivering from fear *and* excitement at being so close to solving the mystery. *"What if all the poisonings were actually spider bites?"*

"Why are we still whispering?" asked Heck.

"Because we don't want the spider to hear us," I said. "Wait—do spiders have ears?"

Heck and I moved closer together, looking all around us for the spider. It could have been anywhere.

"Guys, look at this," mumbled Santos.

We followed his voice around a corner and found him wobbling on his feet like a giraffe that had been shot with a tranquilizer dart. Then I saw what he was looking at: a huge glass enclosure labeled SPIDER COLONY.

The door on this one was also open—and it was empty, too.

But that wasn't the worst part.

The worst part was the body of a woman on the floor in front of it. I'm no expert in dead bodies, but it looked—and smelled—like she had been dead for at least a week. She was wearing blue scrubs and a white lab coat, and her face and arms were covered with purple, swollen spider bites.

Her job must have been taking care of this nightmarish creepy-crawly collection. A tray had fallen on the floor next to her and white plastic containers were scattered all around.

Heck started picked them up and looking inside. "Crickets…mealworms…ew, cockroaches! They're spider food, I guess."

What had happened here?

"Maybe she got bitten by the Brazilian wandering spider and then collapsed when she opened this cage," I guessed. "And all these spiders got out and finished the job."

Santos was still stumbling around. It looked like he was about to fall over.

"Don't pass out!" I warned him.

"Okay," he slurred.

Then his eyes crossed and he fell backward into a rack of glass cages. It teetered…tottered…and toppled over with a CRASH.

Suddenly, the floor was covered with writhing, wriggling snakes.

chapter 65

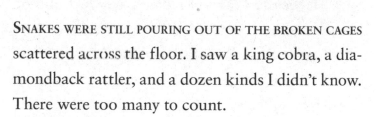

SNAKES WERE STILL POURING OUT OF THE BROKEN CAGES scattered across the floor. I saw a king cobra, a diamondback rattler, and a dozen kinds I didn't know. There were too many to count.

"WAKE UP!" I yelled at Santos, but he was out cold. He had no way of knowing he was about to be covered by a scaly, hissing carpet of serpents.

Heck and I grabbed his ankles and dragged him away from danger, but the repulsive reptiles were between us and the door. When we reached the back wall, we were going to run out of room.

Even worse, the snakes were now slithering after us with their tongues darting in and out.

"Those things are hungry!" yelped Heck. "I wonder how long it's been since they had anything to eat?"

Then I saw a big, old-fashioned table that was being used as a desk.

"We need to get him up on that," I told Heck.

Dropping Santos's feet, we swept books and papers onto the floor, then lifted him by his armpits. He was so heavy we could barely get him off the ground.

"One...two...THREE!" I counted.

We both heaved until we got his head and shoulders on the table. I held him there while Heck lifted his legs. We jumped up after him just as the big cobra hissed and struck at my shoes.

I felt its fangs hit the rubber sole of my sneaker but luckily, they bounced off.

Now we were completely surrounded. The snakes circled the table like they were trying to figure out how to come up and get us.

"Let's make a run for it," said Heck. "They probably won't bite both of us."

"But what happens to the one they *do* bite?" I asked.

"Whoever *isn't* bitten can keep running and get help," said Heck.

"That's a terrible idea," I said. "And besides, we can't leave Santos behind. We should wait for Detective Taylor. As soon as he gets my note, he'll come rescue us."

"What if he hasn't gotten your note?!?"

I pulled out my phone and texted him: In the penthouse. Solved the case. Come get us ASAP or THE SNAKES WILL!!!

We needed to wake Santos up. Bending down, I pinched him, but nothing happened. His eyelids didn't even flutter when I slapped him on both cheeks! I wished more than anything that I had smelling salts like Big Joan and Little John.

That gave me an idea.

Inhaling as deeply as I could, I gulped the air down and let my nervous stomach do the rest. Then I put my mouth right next to Santos's nose.

When I belched in his face, a bullfrog with gastric reflux couldn't have done it any better.

Santos's eyes popped open. He took one look at me—*then balled his fist and swung right at my head!*

chapter 66

THIS IS IT, I THOUGHT. SANTOS HAS FINALLY SNAPPED.

And could I blame him? I was the one who had talked him into joining Detective Club and then brought him along on adventures that he had *told* me were too scary for him. It was a miracle he hadn't picked me up and dunked me in a garbage can already.

(I know that's a lot to think about while someone is swinging their fist at your face, but my mind works faster than most people's.)

I closed my eyes and braced for impact. Getting punched wasn't even the worst thing that could happen. I mean, we were about to get bitten to death by poisonous snakes. How could things get any worse than *that*?

I was about to find out.

Santos did not punch me in the face. His fist whistled over my head—then I heard a soft SPLAT.

"I think I'm gonna barf," said Heck.

When I opened my eyes, Santos was staring at his hand. His fingers were covered with the gooey, pulverized remains of a huge, hairy spider.

"It was about to land on your head," he said. "I just hit it without thinking."

"In that case, try not to think until we get out of this place, because you probably just saved my life," I told him. "But where did the spider come from?"

We all looked up.

And for once, I was too scared to even burp.

The chandelier over our heads was covered with so many spiderwebs that it looked like a family-sized serving of vanilla cotton candy. And the whole thing was crawling with hundreds of spiders of all sizes—like the entire spider colony had taken a vote and decided, *Hey, let's all move to the chandelier over the table!*

The silky thread dangling over my head had been snapped off when Santos punched the spider out of existence.

But a lot *more* spiders were starting to rappel down, too.

"Do you still want to wait here for Detective Taylor?" asked Heck.

"Do you still want to run through those snakes?" I asked him back.

New snakes were still arriving on the floor below us. I guess word was spreading about the free midnight snack: us.

Then a snake's head popped up above the top of the table like a periscope. Its cold black eyes zeroed in on us as its forked tongue flicked in and out, tasting the air.

The snakes were winding their way up the table legs!

"*Please* punch that thing, too," I begged Santos.

He shook his head. "It's too late—I already thought about it. I can only do something brave and stupid if I *don't* think about it."

We were doomed, so I took out my notebook. I

wanted to write everything down before I died, so at least my excellent detective work wouldn't go to waste.

Then Heck stepped to the edge of the table.

"What are you doing?" I asked.

"I'm going to walk out of here," said my brother.

I had always known I was smarter than my brother. Finally, I had proof.

chapter 67

THIS TIME, IT SEEMED LIKE HECK WAS THE ONE LOSING his mind.

"*Walk* out of here? Through the *snakes*?" I asked him.

"Not on my feet," he said. "Watch!"

There were chairs around the table. As we all inched away from the climbing snake, whose head was now sweeping back and forth on the tabletop, Heck stepped down and stood with his feet on the seats of two different chairs. Grabbing one of the chair backs with his uninjured arm, he lifted the chair and moved it forward. Then he did the same thing with the other chair.

If he kept moving, he could make it over the snakes to the door!

"See? It's just like walking on stilts," said Heck.

"That's a brilliant solution," I said as he slowly clomped away from us. "Except for one teeny, tiny problem."

"What's that?" he asked.

"There are only two chairs left."

Heck stopped. I could see him doing the math as he looked back at Santos and me. If each person needed two chairs to use as stilts, then one of us was going to be stranded on Snake and Spider Island.

"I guess that could be a problem," said Heck, who has never been mistaken for Albert Einstein.

The spiders were going to start landing on us any second. The snake had wriggled its entire body onto the top of the table. More snake heads were popping up at all four corners.

Then Santos stepped down onto one of the remaining two chairs.

"Are you *seriously* leaving without me?" I

asked. "I know I got you into this, even though you don't like scary stuff, and I'm *sorry*, but—wait, WHAT ARE YOU DOING?"

Santos grabbed me by the waist, lifted me up in the air, and put me down on the chair next to him. It was crowded, but I was happy to be closer to Santos than to the snake, which was making a beeline across the table toward us. (Or would that have been a *snakeline*?)

Then Santos picked up the final chair, swung it toward Heck, and set it down. He stepped onto it and helped me across.

I finally understood: he was using the two chairs as stepping stones, only each time we stepped *off* a stepping stone, he brought it along with us.

"This is some excellent problem-solving," I told Santos. "See what you can accomplish if you put your mind to it? Just remember, don't think about the—"

"*Shut up!*" said Santos, stopping me before I could say *snakes*.

Which was also smart. Because if he fainted again and fell off, we were both goners.

As Heck worked his way toward the door, Santos and I followed. We stepped onto one chair before moving the other one ahead, keeping just above the squirming snakes on the floor. Santos's long, strong arms made it look easy.

When I looked back at the table, it was completely covered with snakes and spiders. One of the snakes actually opened its mouth and *ate* one of the spiders! Unfortunately, there wasn't enough time to let them kill each other off.

Ahead of us, Heck had gotten the hang of stilt walking and couldn't resist trying a few tricks.

"Check this out, guys!" he said.

First, he hopped from side to side, balancing his chairs on two legs. Then he balanced a chair on one leg and twirled around.

Then he fell down.

Are all younger brothers this predictable, or is it only mine?

"Ow! My wrist!" yelped Heck. He was sitting on the floor, holding his right wrist—the one he hadn't sprained—with his left hand—the one he already had.

"Forget about that and *run*!" I yelled.

Because right behind him was a squirming, rolling ball of snakes!

chapter 68

HECK WAS STILL STARING AT HIS NEWLY SPRAINED RIGHT wrist, like his biggest worry in the world was not being able to climb a ladder or ride a bike. He hadn't even seen the squirming pile of snakes that was now unwinding itself like a demonic ball of string.

Santos moved the empty chair a few feet closer to Heck, lifted me onto it, and then stepped over. He moved the empty chair forward again. Santos was so focused on what he was doing that he didn't even seem to realize Heck was in danger.

"We'll never reach him in time!" I said.

But Santos *had* noticed. The next time he picked me up, he didn't put me down on the chair—he bent his legs, cocked his arms, and *threw* me!

I was so surprised to find myself flying through the air that I let out a high-pitched scream. I sounded like a firework streaking through the sky...just before it explodes.

"AAAAAAAAAAAAAA—"

I flew toward Heck.

"AAAAAAAAAAAAAA—"

I flew *over* Heck.

"AAAAAAAAAAAAAAH—OW!"

BOOM! I landed on the floor. And because the floor was waxed and polished, I slid like a hockey puck on an ice rink—right past the unspooling ball of snakes.

When I looked up, Santos was stilt walking, taking huge steps with his ridiculously long legs. He reached Heck in no time at all.

By now, Heck had seen the snakes—and let's just say he wasn't worried about his wrist anymore.

Santos obviously hadn't stopped to think about what he was doing, because he was acting like he was born to fight snakes. Hopping onto the floor, he picked up one of the chairs and held it like a lion tamer. Scooping up the nearest snake with the chair's legs, he flung it away. It hit the wall like a giant spaghetti noodle—only, unlike a spaghetti noodle, it didn't stick.

The next time, he got TWO snakes at once!

(They didn't stick, either.)

I ran over, grabbed a spare chair, and began doing the same thing, scooping up snakes and flinging them away just as fast as I could. I felt like a snake farmer. Or a snake tamer. Or a snake-annihilating superhero.

Heck couldn't pick up a chair with his injured wrists, so he crawled backward until he was safely behind us.

"Yeah! Roast those reptiles! Sauté those serpents!" he yelled.

I glanced back at him. *"Really?"*

"I'm trying to encourage you," he said sheepishly. "But I'm also hungry, because we didn't eat anything."

Suddenly, there were no more snakes threatening us. We had a clear path to the door.

"What are we waiting for?" I said. "Let's go!"

Santos looked at me. He looked at the chair in his hands. Then he looked at the dozens of snakes he had thrown across the room.

It finally sank in. His knees started knocking so hard I was amazed he could run at all. But we sprinted out of the Zoo of Death, through the penthouse apartment, and out the front door, slamming it shut behind us.

The nightmare was over.

Almost.

chapter 69

OUTSIDE THE PENTHOUSE, WE STOOD WITH OUR BACKS to the door. We were breathing so hard it was like we had just completed every single event in the Olympics.

"Did that really just happen or did we all have the exact same hallucination?" asked Heck.

"I wish we had only imagined it," groaned Santos.

"You were amazing!" I told him. "You know, I can't believe *I'm* saying this, but maybe your problem is that sometimes you just think too much."

"I'd have to think about that," he said.

"Seriously—don't," I said.

As I looked down at the chessboard floor, I saw a shiny black spider tiptoeing up the heel of my sneaker. I shook it off, only to see two more spiders crawling on my other sneaker. I scraped *those* off with my toe.

A chill tingled from my heels to the roots of my hair as I forced myself to turn around.

More spiders were spilling out from under the door. Two, then four—then ten, then twenty, until they became a flood of legs, fangs, and tiny black eyes. We stood frozen in terror as hundreds of spiders—some black and shiny, others brown and hairy—boiled over the transom, around the door's sides, and even through its old-fashioned keyhole.

Heck screamed.

Santos wobbled.

I said, "Time to go," and ran.

"You don't have to tell me twice," said Heck, who was somehow already ahead of me.

Fortunately, Santos didn't faint this time. We raced to the elevator and pressed the button—but it had moved to a lower floor, and there was no other way out. To reach the fire stairs, we would have had to go over the spiders and back through the snake-infested penthouse.

Waves of spiders scurried across the floor toward us while we waited for the elevator to come back. Heck picked up the vase with the peacock feathers and threw it at them. I tore down the green velvet curtains and tried to sweep them away. Santos flipped over the table. Even though we managed to squish some of the spiders, more just kept coming.

"We could sure use a Molotov cocktail right now!" said Heck, and for once, I agreed with my brother.

Finally, the elevator arrived. While I pulled the door open, Santos raised his leg and stomped the nearest spider with a size twelve sneaker. There were so many, and they were coming so fast, that before I knew it, he was clog dancing on them, smashing as many as he could while Heck and I escaped.

"Come on!" I yelled as Heck shoved past me.

Santos hopscotched his way into the elevator—flattening even more spiders on the way—and I yanked the door shut and pressed the button. He continued stomping as spiders came through the cage-like door until finally there was nothing left moving on the floor.

Then a spider dropped onto Heck's back from the ceiling. Without thinking, I punched it as hard as I could.

"Ouch!" yelled Heck.

"Spider," I explained.

"I'll bet," he said, unable to see the bug guts on his shirt.

We crowded into a corner as the elevator started to drop. Santos took off one sneaker and held it above his head, ready to use it like a flyswatter if any more spiders attacked from above.

I watched the ceiling so hard my eyeballs hurt, but as the floors fell away and no more spiders appeared, I finally began to relax. When we passed the second floor and reached the lobby, I sighed in relief.

But because we had all been looking up, none of us had seen what was waiting for us in the atrium.

chapter 70

WE WALKED OUT INTO COMPLETE CHAOS. BUILDING residents were being herded toward the front door by uniformed police officers. I saw Fred Frizzell wearing a bathrobe, holding a chihuahua in one hand and pulling a suitcase with the other. The bodybuilder was carrying a duffel bag—*he* slept in *Star Wars* pajamas. And the old lady who had bought Heck's cookies was nervously nibbling one of them as she shuffled toward the door.

A small army of people rushed into the building, all of them covered from head to toe in white hazmat suits. All of them were carrying tools, from snake hooks and cages to high-tech vacuum cleaners that must have been designed for catching spiders.

Detective Taylor pushed his way through the crowd.

"We're evacuating the building," he told us. "We finally ID'd the poison: spider venom."

I couldn't help it—I started laughing. I laughed so loud and for so long that Detective Taylor started to look worried.

"You'd better start on the top floor," I finally said. "What took you so long?"

CASE FILES

Name: Lothar and Ursula Ernst

Occupation: World travelers and ????

Relationship to case: They started it.

Hair, eyes, age, etc.: I've never seen them, so I have no idea what they look like. This picture is just a guess.

Identifying characteristics: Look, I already said I've never seen them, OK?

Personality: I think they don't like people very much. Just a guess.

Habits, behavior & special talents: They like to travel to far-off places. But they don't bring back T-shirts or any other NORMAL souvenirs.

WHO ARE THEY???

DETECTIVE'S NOTES:

I am not a criminal profiler, but after examining their home, I have made the following deductions:

* They have more money than they know what to do with
* Which is why they spend it on bizarre things nobody needs to have in their home
* And it's a mystery to me why they even bother decorating their home
* Because they never seem to be in it
* But that's also probably why they don't have a normal pet, like a cat or a dog
* When they get back from wherever the heck they are now, they're going to have a BIG surprise waiting for them!

chapter 71

I SAT ACROSS FROM KERMIT AT THE MARBLE-TOPPED chess table in the wood-paneled lounge of the Arcanum. We were playing a little bit more slowly than usual—we weren't even using a clock.

But that didn't mean I wasn't trying to win.

I moved a bishop forward, trapping Kermit's rook. I was closing in on his king.

Kermit lifted a pawn and stroked his beard, deep in thought.

It was Sunday, a week and a half after Detective Club had solved the case. Kermit had recovered quickly after finally being injected with antivenom. He still looked weak, but his mind was just as sharp as it used to be.

"You have been practicink," Kermit said as he put the pawn down.

I moved a knight toward the center of the board. "You gave me a good chess puzzle while you were in the hospital."

Kermit chuckled. "I vas delirious, vaking only few moments at time. Playink Spider Attack vas lucky idea."

Detective Taylor told me the doctors had completely missed the bite marks in the first victims. Kermit's was covered by his bushy beard. Serenity *swallowed* a spider in her yogurt. Mr. Park was bitten between his toes by a spider hiding in his slipper. Only Oskar had an easy-to-spot bite with obvious swelling.

And Bizzy? She managed to get bitten *inside her ear*—we still hadn't figured out how that happened. Fortunately, she was completely fine after also getting antivenom.

Kermit defended with a pawn and I captured it with my knight. He captured back, but that was part of my plan.

Just a few more moves and the old geezer was mine.

After evacuating the building, Detective Taylor's team had searched every nook and cranny until they were sure they had found every last one of the missing spiders and snakes. We had all been back home in forty-eight hours.

Except for my parents, of course. They had just landed in Los Angeles when they learned the mystery was solved—so naturally, they turned around and flew right back to Australia.

They had "unfinished business," they told us. Does that sound like professor talk to you? Heck is more convinced than ever that they're secret agents and says he's going to prove it.

Nobody can find Lothar and Ursula Ernst. If you ask me, they're searching the world for even more poisonous critters. But they're in for a big surprise when they get back. They're going to be arrested and charged with involuntary manslaughter—not to mention ivory smuggling.

It was time to close my trap on Kermit. I moved my rook, putting his king in check. He moved his king, but he was running out of room.

Amazing Andy was also missing. That was my fault—I forgot to take the paperclips back—but Detective Taylor didn't seem bothered.

"Don't worry, he'll turn up," he'd told me. "Probably at another birthday party."

Maybe Heck's, I thought.

I needed to stop letting my mind wander and focus on finishing the game. Kermit was staring at me, probably waiting for me to move.

"Spider...attack," said Kermit softly.

"No, that's *your* thing," I told him. "I just made this attack up as I went along."

I lifted my queen.

Something was wrong with Kermit. He seemed frozen, and beads of sweat were breaking out on his face.

Then I looked down at the board.

Right in the middle was a brown spider as big as Kermit's hand. Its front two legs were raised like it was angry and ready to bite. Thanks to our night in the penthouse, I now knew exactly what kind it was.

A Brazilian wandering spider.

Extremely aggressive—and deadly.

Somehow, Detective Taylor's team had missed it. But I wasn't going to let it bite Kermit. Or me.

I didn't think. I just smashed the queen down on the spider's head, grinding it back and forth and squishing it into the board.

The spider's legs twitched a few times and then it stopped moving.

"Checkmate!" I said.

"You vin again," said Kermit, wiping his forehead with a wrinkled handkerchief.

"I faced down a whole army of poisonous spiders," I told him as I let go of the chess piece. "It's going to take more than one to stop Minerva Keen, Detective!"

ABOUT THE AUTHORS

◇◇◇

For his prodigious imagination and championship of literacy in America, **JAMES PATTERSON** was awarded the 2019 National Humanities Medal, and he has also received the Literarian Award for Outstanding Service to the American Literary Community from the National Book Foundation. He holds the Guinness World Record for the most #1 *New York Times* bestsellers, including *Max Einstein, Middle School, I Funny,* and *Jacky Ha-Ha,* and his books have sold more than 400 million copies worldwide. A tireless champion of the power of books and reading, Patterson created a children's book imprint, JIMMY Patterson, whose mission is simple: "We want every kid who finishes a JIMMY book to say, 'PLEASE GIVE ME ANOTHER BOOK.'" He has donated more than three million books to students and soldiers and funds over four hundred Teacher and Writer Education Scholarships at twenty-one colleges and universities. He also supports forty thousand school libraries and has donated millions of dollars to independent bookstores. Patterson invests proceeds from the sales of JIMMY Patterson Books in pro-reading initiatives.

KEIR GRAFF is thrilled to collaborate with James Patterson on the Minerva Keen series. His funny and fantastical middle-grade adventure novels include *The Tiny Mansion, The Phantom Tower* (a *Chicago Tribune* Best Children's Book), and *The Matchstick Castle* (an official Illinois Reads selection). He lives in Chicago.

MIDDLE SCHOOL

- The Worst Years of My Life
- Get Me Out of Here!
- Big Fat Liar
- How I Survived Bullies, Broccoli, and Snake Hill
- Ultimate Showdown
- Save Rafe!
- Just My Rotten Luck
- Dog's Best Friend
- Escape to Australia
- From Hero to Zero
- Born to Rock
- Master of Disaster
- Field Trip Fiasco
- It's a Zoo in Here!
- Winter Blunderland

TREASURE HUNTERS

- Treasure Hunters
- Danger Down the Nile
- Secret of the Forbidden City
- Peril at the Top of the World
- Quest for the City of Gold
- All-American Adventure
- The Plunder Down Under
- The Ultimate Quest
- The Greatest Treasure Hunt

MIDDLE GRADE FICTION

- Becoming Muhammad Ali (cowritten with Kwame Alexander)
- Best Nerds Forever
- Laugh Out Loud
- Minerva Keen's Detective Club
- Not So Normal Norbert
- Pottymouth and Stoopid
- Public School Superhero
- Scaredy Cat
- Unbelievably Boring Bart
- Word of Mouse

MAX EINSTEIN

- The Genius Experiment
- Rebels with a Cause
- Max Einstein Saves the Future
- World Champions!

For exclusives, trailers, and
more about the books, visit
Kids.JamesPatterson.com.